A

Gates, Doris
The Cat and Mrs. Cary

Date Due

A-2 NOV 35			
APR 23 1973 F-1			
MAR 2 8 1974 X			
MAR 2 6 1975 B			
MAY 2 9 1980 EL			
APR 2 2 1990 A1			
MAY 0 4 1990 A1			

c.1 ✓ 7982

Mrs. Cary expects life in Crow's Harbor to be quiet and peaceful. In this she is disappointed. First she acquires a talking cat, then her nephew comes for a visit. After that there is one adventure after another—walking ghosts, secret doors and smugglers.

THE CAT
AND
MRS. CARY

THE CAT
AND
MRS. CARY

BY DORIS GATES
Illustrated by Peggy Bacon

THE VIKING PRESS · NEW YORK

PRINTED IN THE U.S.A. BY MURRAY PRINTING CO.

To Gordon M. Wheeler

Who always asked, "How's the book?"
and waited for the answer.

CONTENTS

THE CAT
AND
MRS. CARY

1

MRS. CARY
TAKES A BET

"It won't do a bit of good."

Mrs. Cary, on her knees beside the fishpond, lifted her hands from the water and glanced toward the road. She was sure the voice had come from that direction. She could see no one, however. Sitting back on her heels, she peered between the fence stakes that enclosed the garden of Three Corners. The fence was a friendly one, its stakes set conveniently far apart to allow anyone to come through—anyone, that is, smaller than a horse or a cow.

Still squatting on her heels, she lifted her head to peer at the cypresses stretching their dark branches high above the pool. No one there, either. A squirrel's excited scolding sounded suddenly from the pine across the garden. Mrs. Cary listened carefully for a moment, then shook her head. The voice had been quite different from the squirrel's.

She tipped forward onto her knees again and bent to her work. I must have dreamed that voice, she decided.

Yet there it was again! "It won't do a bit of good, I say."
Slowly Mrs. Cary got to her feet.

It was then she saw the cat.

He was sitting just beyond the fence, a thin and scraggly-
looking creature having almost as many colors as a patchwork
quilt. Mostly he was a mixture of brownish gray, with a dab
of white under his chin. Just now a shaft of sunlight caught
his ears, revealing against their thin and glowing cartilage
dark streaks which were the cat's campaign ribbons.

For several seconds he returned Mrs. Cary's scrutiny; then
he lifted one paw and quickly gave his nose a wipe with it.

Incredible as it seemed, she could have sworn she saw him
smile around that paw.

"It couldn't have been you who spoke just now," she said in
a tone of amazement and more to herself than to the cat.

"None other," he replied.

Mrs. Cary backed slowly until she could feel the edge of
the old garden seat beside the pond. She lowered herself

carefully onto it, never once taking her eyes from the cat.

A good many things were rocketing through her mind. Since she had only lived here for two weeks, and since it was the first time in her life she had ever lived in an old house in an old garden beside the sea, she had, of course, expected that there would be many changes and adjustments to be made in her way of life. She had accepted the fact that she would have to walk to the village a mile away. A battered bus carried passengers between Crow's Harbor and the nearest town, Kingsmount, four miles over the hill. But there were no bus routes within the village itself, and she didn't feel she could afford a car. She was beginning to understand that neighborliness here took a different form from the one it had assumed in the big city she had come from. Here neighbors didn't keep themselves *to* themselves the same. She had learned to put her house key under the mat instead of carrying it with her. "Suppose you left something on the stove?" Mrs. Melton had reasoned. "How would anyone get inside to turn it off?"—a question which Mrs. Cary found herself unable to answer and which branded as idiotic any thought of *not* leaving the key under the mat. She had found the limited offerings of the local Bookmobile a sharp contrast to the rich store of the big-city library. Still, the Bookmobile would deliver anything she asked for on its next trip. So that wasn't so bad.

But this beat anything. A talking cat! It was even more remarkable than the mysterious disappearance of her goldfish.

Three days ago Mrs. Cary had cleaned out the fishpond and slipped six goldfish into its expectant waters. They were rather large goldfish and had cost sixty-five cents apiece. This was unquestionably a high price, but when she saw them flashing in the dark water she hadn't regretted her extravagance. They were like chips of sunlight in the pool's murky depths. Suddenly the dissheveled old fishpond had become the nicest part of the garden.

Then the fish began to disappear. The first morning after she had planted them, there were only five. The second morning there were four. This morning there had been just three. So this morning Mrs. Cary had asked her neighbors, when they met at their row of mailboxes, what she should do to save her fish.

"Raccoons are getting them," declared Mrs. Melton.

This was possible, since Three Corners was on the wild side of the village, between the sea and the marsh. Then how did one discourage the raccoons? Mrs. Melton didn't know.

"It's a cat," affirmed Major Paddleford, who lived just up the road in the Willoughby guest house. "It's an old fishing Tom. I've seen one hanging around here."

Then how could one outwit the fishing Tom? The major's answers were not very helpful.

"Kingfishers will take them, too," offered Mrs. Kane.

Then how did one overcome kingfishers? Mrs. Kane had no answer.

"Better forget all about having fish," advised the major finally.

"A pond is nothing without fish in it," declared Mrs. Cary.

Later that same morning the grocer's boy came through the garden on his way to the kitchen with the weekly grocery order.

"What do you suppose is getting my goldfish?" Mrs. Cary asked him, just as she had asked the others.

The grocer's boy wagged his head, puzzled.

"Search me, ma'am," he said finally. "But I can tell you what to do."

"What?" asked Mrs. Cary.

The grocer's boy scratched his head. "Well," he began, "one thing's sure. Whatever's gettin' them goldfish is gettin' them *out of the water*. Right?"

"Right," answered Mrs. Cary.

"Then cover the water," said the grocer's boy.

So this very afternoon Mrs. Cary had walked to the village and had bought a roll of chicken wire and carried it home under her arm. It was while she was spreading it out across the pool that the voice had spoken to her.

Now she stared at the cat and decided to put a question directly to him. "Why do you say 'It won't do a bit of good'?"

A conceited look settled on the cat's face. "When it comes to catching fish, you've never seen anything to match my equal."

Mrs. Cary was too amazed by this declaration to be bothered by its syntax. "So it *is* a cat that's been getting them!" she cried. "Major Paddleford was right after all."

"Not *a* cat, *the* cat," The Cat corrected her, scratching behind an ear.

"Well, you won't get any more," she told him.

He abruptly left off scratching, rose to his feet, and slipped into the garden between the fence stakes. When he had come to within a few feet of the pool, he sat down again. This time there could be no doubt about his smile.

"Want to bet? I'll give odds."

Mrs. Cary was not a betting woman. She had been reared to believe that all gambling was a sin and couldn't have figured odds to save her life. Though she enjoyed a game of canasta now and then and had once tried to learn contract bridge, she took small interest in games of any kind. Now, however, she saw in the cat's offer a chance to strike a bargain with him. Gambling for the lives of her three remaining goldfish could hardly be a sin!

"What odds?" she asked, hoping she was saying the right thing.

"If you can keep me away from those last three goldfish tonight, I'll not only let them alone forever, I'll keep any other animal from catching them. And that's about as odd as anything can get."

"And if you do catch them?"

"I'll just go on being the most expensively fed cat in Christendom."

"I'll take your bet," said Mrs. Cary, feeling rather daring.

"I'd make you shake hands on it," said The Cat, "only somebody's coming up the road. Whoever it is might see us, and you're a newcomer, don't forget. If I know your neighbors, and I think I do, that's already one strike against you. No use making it two sooner than necessary. And keep quiet about the bet."

As if I wouldn't, thought Mrs. Cary just as Major Paddleford came into sight around one of the three corners of the garden. In a twinkling The Cat was through the fence and across the road. There he paused for a quick look back before slipping into Mrs. Melton's garden and out of sight.

Major Paddleford took his hat clear off his head as he came abreast of the pool and Mrs. Cary. "How-de-do," he shouted as if giving a command on a parade ground. The major, though many years retired, had never lost his military bearing. He walked as if he were inspecting a line of troops. His shoulders were always squared (padded, Mrs. Cary thought), and he set his feet down firmly, as if warning the ground that he would tolerate no nonsense from it. He was never without a walking stick, which he swung so vigorously that its cane sides flashed even on a foggy day. His thick white eyebrows bristled above his keen blue eyes, and his short white mustache was like a third eyebrow set by mistake under his big nose.

"Just saw a cat slip across the road," boomed the major. "That's the one I was telling you about." He took a slice at the air with his stick. "Take my word for it, dear lady, that's the varmint that's getting your goldfish."

Mrs. Cary smiled sociably at him. "I believe you're right, Major. But I think I've found a way to best him."

"How's that?" queried the major, coming up to the fence. The stakes were not nearly far enough apart to allow him to get through.

"I'm covering the pool with this chicken wire," she explained. "I think if I roll it across from here to here"—pointing—"and then weight it with rocks, the cat can't get under."

"M-m-m-m-m," the major mused, now leaning on the fence. From this distance he cast a critical eye over her handiwork. At last he said, "I think it would be better if you were to sink the ends of the wire in a trench."

"Perhaps," said Mrs. Cary. "But that would make the pool look dreadful."

"True," agreed the major cheerfully, "but it's the only thing to do. If you bury the ends of the wire and weight the sides, the cat can't possibly get his paws under to fish."

Mrs. Cary tweaked the stubborn wire irritably. Suddenly this old house, its three-cornered garden, the fishpond, The Cat, and the major—all of it had become a bore.

"It all seems such a nuisance," she said.

"I quite agree, dear lady," said the major affably. "It would be much simpler just to shoot the cat. If I may say so, I'm not a bad marksman. At your service any time." He ran a quick finger across his mustache.

"I've always heard it was bad luck to kill a cat," Mrs. Cary countered.

The major chuckled tolerantly. "Bad luck for the cat, no doubt. However, in this case, I think the cat would be better off dead. He's mangy and starving."

"I think he might be better off fed," returned Mrs. Cary.

"He'll be fed all right, unless you take my advice."

With which the major backed away from the fence, lifted his hat, swung his cane, and paced off down the road.

After only a moment's consideration, Mrs. Cary dropped to her knees and began burying the wire exactly as the major had directed.

2

OUT OF
THE NIGHT

Later, her labors at the pool ended, Mrs. Cary was having her dinner from a tray in front of the fireplace. Usually she sat properly at the dining table with two candles lighting her plate and a record playing on the hi-fi. Though she lived alone, and had ever since her husband's death two years ago, Mrs. Cary had never "let herself go," believing that a life without form and pattern was no life at all.

Today, however, The Cat had somewhat changed the pattern for her. Engrossed in outsmarting him, she had not been aware of the passage of time. The dinner hour had crept up on her before she was quite finished. By the time she had completed setting the wire, she was so bone-tired and so nearly famished that the intricate ballet of dinner as usual held no delights at all. Thankful for the remnants of a roast, she made a sandwich. Still rummaging, she found a cold artichoke which would do beautifully for a salad. She put the two leftovers on separate plates, then made a cup of instant coffee. This was as good a barometer of her culinary abandon as one could wish. Next she put the three items on a tray and carried the tray into the living room, where she placed it carefully on the hospitality table in front of the sofa. She seated herself and let her head rest against the sofa back while she enjoyed the billowy comfort of its soft cushions. At last she sighed, straightened up, and reached for the sandwich. Without bothering to spread the paper napkin, she took a big bite and began munching happily.

It was then she heard the tapping.

She tried to tell herself it was a twig hitting against the window, but every instinct told her differently. There was a rhythm to this tapping. It went tap-tap-a-tap. Tap-tap-a-tap. No twig ever tapped like that, not even at Three Corners. She looked toward the window, half fearing what she was sure she would see. For several seconds she watched until her eyes had grown sufficiently accustomed to the dark beyond the pane to focus on the object waiting there. Without surprise, Mrs. Cary at last saw a cat's face peering in at her.

Replacing the sandwich, she rose and crossed the room. It was a casement window, and for a moment Mrs. Cary had difficulty with the latch, which was somewhat rusted. This gave The Cat time to cross the wide sill to avoid being knocked into the garden when at last she succeeded in swinging the window open.

"The bet's off," he announced, his eyes blazing and his ears flat.

"Why?" asked Mrs. Cary, shivering as a gust from the sea swept past her to the fireplace, which immediately sent a puff of smoke into the room.

"I happened to hear Major Henry Paddleford, U.S.A. Retired, holding forth this afternoon on how to fix your fishpond. Somehow I had too much confidence in your sporting blood to believe that you'd follow his advice. I find I overrated you. Well, I want you to know, as of right now, that I didn't bet you *and* the military that you could keep me from getting those fool goldfish. The bet was between you and me."

Mrs. Cary glanced away from The Cat to the hospitality table, where her coffee was cooling in the draft from the open window.

"Won't you come in so that we may discuss this more comfortably?" she asked.

The Cat had hardly expected a courteous return of his blast. His eyes narrowed a little and his whiskers twitched as he tried to recover the advantage.

"So you can lay a trap for me?" he snarled at last.

Mrs. Cary bristled. "I'm truly sorry if I failed to abide by whatever is considered sporting in a bet between a woman and a cat—" she began.

"*The* Cat," corrected that animal.

She ignored the correction. "But I can assure you that taking advantage of anyone invited inside my house would be as far from my mind as—as—well, as anything I could imagine."

The Cat stiffened his ears and peered suspiciously past her into the room. "You alone?"

"Certainly," snapped Mrs. Cary. "Do you suppose I'd be carrying on a conversation with you if I weren't?"

"Not likely, I guess," he admitted and leaped gracefully past her. He landed with a slight thud and proceeded toward the fire, his tail up, his whole manner that of a cat thoroughly at home.

"You've certainly done a lot with this place already," he observed, looking critically about him. He measured the distance to the top of the book-lined shelves flanking each side of the chimney and remarked, "A reader, I see."

Mrs. Cary resumed her place in front of her supper tray, murmuring fatuously, "What's a home without books?"

"Oh, I don't know," returned The Cat easily. "You could be prejudiced." While Mrs. Cary went on alternately munching the sandwich and pulling off artichoke leaves, The Cat studied her thoughtfully. Then he let his gaze again wander around the room as if he were taking careful note of everything in it. "Yes, you've done a lot with this place," he repeated. "I must say it looks a lot better than when Mrs. Crow lived here."

Mrs. Cary smiled around an artichoke leaf, swallowed and said, evidently pleased, "Really? Mrs. Melton takes a different view, or so I interpreted it. *She* said it looked nothing the way it did when poor Mrs. Crow lived here."

"And truer word was never spoken," said The Cat. "It looked like nothing at all when Mrs. Crow lived here. Full of antique sofas covered with horsehair." He threw her a disgusted look. "Did you ever try to snuggle into a horsehair sofa?" Without waiting for an answer, he added, "And this'll kill you. Mrs. Crow wasn't even clean."

"Oh, come now," said Mrs. Cary, who disliked unkind talk of the dead. "I just refuse to believe that. There was nothing to indicate it when I moved in here. The floors and cupboards were in good shape."

"I call any woman dirty who feeds a cat off one saucer day after day and never bothers to wash it between feedings. And that's what Mrs. Crow used to do." The Cat's voice was shrill with indignation. "You may be able to tell a housekeeper by her cupboards, but believe me, cats have a better measure than that. Show me the cat dish, and I'll tell you what kind of a housekeeper a woman is."

This struck Mrs. Cary funny, and she repressed a giggle. "Suppose she doesn't have a cat?"

"So much the worse for her," growled The Cat darkly.

"It occurs to me that you know a good deal about Mrs. Crow," said Mrs. Cary taking a sip of coffee.

Before replying to this, The Cat sat down with his back to the fire and whipped his tail around his front feet. He had a fine sense of timing and he knew Mrs. Cary was in for a shock.

"I was Mrs. Crow's cat." His whiskers twitched with satisfaction at the surprise on Mrs. Cary's face. She couldn't have looked more astonished. "What's so wonderful about that?" he demanded.

"It does seem strange to me that no one ever told me Mrs. Crow had a talking cat. After all, it was I who bought her house."

The Cat lifted his paws and hid his face between them in a fit of laughter. "My dear lady, as the major would say, all cats are talking cats. But not all people can understand them."

"Then Mrs. Crow never understood you?"

"That she didn't. As a matter of fact, you are the only person who has ever understood me." The Cat let these significant words sink in while Mrs. Cary studied him. With the firelight shining around the edges of his fur, he looked much less ugly. She couldn't see any sign of mange, either. "I used to talk by the hour to Mrs. Crow," he went on. "I always tried to talk to her when she was in the kitchen, that being the place where cats naturally talk the best. But all I ever got for my sociability was the business end of the broom. She had some funny notions, did Mrs. Crow." He paused to reminisce a moment. "For one thing, she thought if you gave cats nothing but milk, they would be better hunters." Again he paused to smile wickedly. "They will be, all right. What else can the poor things do? My specialty was the neighborhood goldfish pools."

"Which brings us back to the goldfish," said Mrs. Cary. She had almost finished her supper. "I should like to make a bargain with you."

"I'm willing to listen to any reasonable offer," said The Cat grandly.

"If I agree to feed you well each and every day, will you let my fish alone?"

The Cat fixed her with a long and level look. "Does that mean meat as well as milk, all kinds of meat—liver, heart, beef, *and* chicken?"

"It does," said Mrs. Cary.

The Cat considered this a moment. "On a clean saucer?"

"Certainly on a clean saucer."

"Then it's a deal." With these words he crossed to where she sat and reached up a paw to her. Mrs. Cary took it gravely, surprised to feel how soft it was. And yet, as The Cat drew it back again, she felt the hint of claws below the softness of his pads.

"And now, if it isn't too much trouble—" he began.

Mrs. Cary gave a start and rose from the sofa. "Oh, for heaven's sake!" she exclaimed. "Here I've sat thoughtlessly stuffing myself, while you no doubt are hungry as a starved cat— Oh, I beg your pardon."

"Quite all right," replied The Cat amiably as he followed her into the kitchen.

Some time later, his sides bulging with a mixture of things dear to his appetite, The Cat was sitting in front of the fire, cleaning himself with the utter self-absorption which only a well-fed cat can achieve. Snug in her fireside chair, Mrs. Cary sat reading, her feet only inches away from him.

From outside came the rhythmic beat of the sea along the shore. The somber noise of its constant rush and withdrawal served to accent the peace and stillness within.

Suddenly they were both startled by a rap on the front door. Mrs. Cary lowered her book and snatched off her glasses. The Cat held himself twisted sideways for a moment, his tongue suspended above his fur, his every sense alert.

"I wonder who that can be," said Mrs. Cary.

"There's one sure way to find out," said The Cat, following through on his stroke.

Mrs. Cary rose and went to the door.

3

A MYSTERIOUS CALLER

The house at Three Corners dated back to an age which had respect for shadows. It boasted no picture windows or glass walls. It knew no "planters." Its roof was patched, and its chimney smoked when the wind was in the south. But still it looked a dependable old house, the kind which puts its arms around you and says: "Be comfortable. Rest. I have endured much. I can protect you."

As Mrs. Cary went to open the front door, she had no reason to fear the eyes of any passer-by. Every window was screened by a ragged growth of fuchsias or geraniums. The front entry, to make privacy doubly secure, had no windows at all. It was hardly more than an alcove off the living room, from which the stairs rose to the second story.

In the dim glow of the porch light, opaque from wind and fog, Mrs. Cary saw that a stranger stood on her doorstep.

"Good evening," she said, making a question of the words.

"Evening," returned the stranger. His voice was a deep rumble. "I'm looking for a Mrs. Crow."

"Mrs. Crow used to live here," explained Mrs. Cary, "but she died some time ago. This is my house now."

The man turned to look out the open beams of the little porch, considering her words. At last he turned back to her, his eyes suspicious. "Funny they never told me," he said.

"Yes, it is funny," replied Mrs. Cary, "for she's been dead at least two months."

The stranger turned these words over in his mind before asking, "Mind if I use your phone? I have to get the fellow back who dropped me off here."

"Of course not," she said, drawing back into the entry. "It's right here beside the stairs."

The man followed her in and shut the door.

Mrs. Cary could now see that her caller had iron-gray hair which was thick and curly, that his features were rugged and his skin tanned. He must have been somewhere between fifty-five and sixty and was handsome in a rough way. He was dressed in a blue shirt and blue jeans. On his feet were brogans so stiff and unwieldy they might have been carved out of wood. He moved heavily toward the telephone when Mrs. Cary pointed it out to him, his stiff shoes thumping loudly on the polished floor. A fisherman, she thought, or a pirate.

She tried to imagine what he would look like with a kerchief wrapped round his head and an earring dangling from one ear. Rather like one of Howard Pyle's pirates, she decided, and felt a pleasant shiver go along her spine.

He began speaking into the phone. Since he made no attempt to lower his voice, she found it easy to follow his side of the conversation.

"Joe there?" he demanded. "He isn't? Well, I guess he

hasn't had time to get there yet. Tell him when he comes in that Mo wants him to pick him up at Mrs. Crow's right away. Yes, right away. Yes, I know she's dead. Just found out. But I'm at her old place. You tell Joe to come and get me right away. Okay." He hung up.

"Thanks very much," he said around the corner of the stairs. "I'll be getting along now." His eyes swept the living room and came to rest on The Cat, who was now staring into the fire, indifferent apparently to what went on behind him. "Quite a cat you've got there."

"Yes. He wandered into my garden this afternoon and has quite adopted me."

"That's one way of putting it," said The Cat without taking his eyes off the quietly darting flames that licked the chunks of oak wood.

The stranger chuckled. "Never could learn to like cats,"

he said in a way which gave credit to himself. "Can't stand their yowling. Take dogs, now. I like a good dog."

"But dogs bark," Mrs. Cary reminded him, feeling a stir of loyalty for the friendless creature on her hearth.

"I'll say they do," agreed the stranger heartily, "and that keeps prowlers away. Dogs are good for something. What's a cat good for? You tell me." He flung the challenge good-naturedly.

Mrs. Cary decided to accept it. The Cat was now a member of her household and as such entitled to her support. But how was she to defend him? What on earth was a cat good for? she asked herself. She had never owned a cat; indeed she had always understood that nobody ever owned one. As she searched her memory of all she had ever heard about them, she felt the stranger's grin upon her, daring her to reply.

Suddenly she had it. "They catch mice," she cried.

"And birds," added the man, still with his teasing grin.

"And smugglers," added The Cat, twisting his neck to look at the stranger with blazing topaz eyes.

"Smugglers!" exclaimed Mrs. Cary with a laugh.

Slowly the grin faded from the stranger's face, and his eyes fixed themselves coldly upon her.

"What do you mean, 'smugglers'?"

Now she had done it. She had let something slip which had meaning for him. He was upset; he looked almost frightening.

"You'd better answer me," he said darkly.

"I didn't mean anything," she said faltering. "I meant nothing at all."

"Then why did you say 'smugglers'?"

"Because The Cat said it, I guess." Would he accept this

outlandish explanation as a joke? she wondered hopefully.

"You expect me to believe that?" the man asked.

"No, of course not," returned Mrs. Cary. So he wasn't going to take it as a joke. Well, she'd have to think of something else. She tried a reassuring laugh. "I was only fooling," she confessed lamely. "Just my inept sense of humor, I suppose. It was silly of me."

The man studied her for several seconds, then dropped his gaze to The Cat. He shook his head. "It beats me. That cat growls and right away you say 'smugglers.' Why smugglers, though?" He looked quickly back at her again.

But Mrs. Cary had had enough of it. "I've tried to tell you how it happened. You can take it or leave it. What seems a joke to me evidently isn't a joke to you. It's as simple as that."

Before he could reply, a horn sounded from the road.

"That'll be Joe." He started toward the door, then he paused to say, "I'm sorry if I was rude. Thanks for letting me use the phone."

"You're quite welcome," said Mrs. Cary stiffly.

As he opened the door and stepped outside, she could see the lights of a car slicing the dark at the end of the walk. Suddenly a figure strode through them, swinging a walking stick. He hesitated on the edge of the light as if trying to decide whether or not to come in, and Mrs. Cary held her breath. She had recognized Major Paddleford out for his customary pre-bedtime ramble. "Tucking in the neighborhood," he called it. With another swing of the stick he went on up the road, his footsteps gradually swallowed up in the sound of the sea's swish across the sands below the cliff and the closer panting of the car at the end of the walk.

The stranger, with a parting nod and smile, started toward the car, and Mrs. Cary began to draw the door shut. Before she had quite closed it, a shadow darted through the opening and bounded across the porch. The Cat!

Now what am I supposed to do? she asked herself, peering into the dark beyond the porch. The car was starting to pull away. How will he get in again? I may be upstairs and asleep the next time he comes tapping at the window.

Feeling somewhat annoyed, she returned to the living room, put a record on the hi-fi, and sat down by the fire. What an evening it had been! And what a day! From talking cats to suspicious strangers, Mrs. Cary reviewed it carefully and could find little sense in it anywhere—unless, of course, she had at last found a way to secure the safety of her goldfish. Right now, with The Cat somewhere outside and presumably on the prowl, this last didn't seem positively guaranteed. How reliable was The Cat anyway?

When it was time for bed, she went into the kitchen and stuck her head out the back door. "Kitty, kitty, kitty," she called. But no scrawny form came bounding through the petunias. No patch of calico sat cleaning its shirtfront on the flagstones leading down under the cypresses.

"He can jolly well stay outside," muttered Mrs. Cary, slamming the door shut. "And if he thinks I'm going to crawl downstairs later on to let him in, he's very much mistaken."

She returned to the living room, put the screen in front of the fire, picked up her book and glasses, turned off all the lights except the one over the stairs, and went up to her bedroom.

Settling herself against her pillows a few minutes later, she happily opened her book and began to read. But after only a page or two she put it down and removed her glasses. It was no use. Only a small part of her mind was focusing on her book. Most of it was still dwelling on The Cat and what he might be up to. Could she trust him to keep his part of their bargain, or was he even now crouched on the edge of the goldfish pond? For two cents she'd go down and see. Then she smiled, remembering. The wire screening was still over the water! And The Cat had practically admitted that he couldn't get under it. So there was nothing to worry about after all.

She placed her book on the night stand and snapped off the light. For a little while she listened to the voice of the sea filling the night beyond her windows. A mighty wave smacked the beach, making the old house shudder.

The tide is coming in, Mrs. Cary thought sleepily, and slept.

4

THE CAT'S SUSPICIONS

Mrs. Cary wasted no time in getting out to the goldfish pond next morning. She dressed hurriedly, skimmed downstairs, and passed through the kitchen with only a glance at the coffee pot. Breakfast could wait, for once.

Straight to the pool she went and bent eagerly over its screened surface. A golden flash rewarded her scrutiny, then another, and another. The fish were all there!

"You have a trusting nature, I see."

Mrs. Cary whirled. There sat The Cat, his tail wrapped snugly around his front feet, eying her disgustedly.

"When I make a bargain, I make a bargain," he informed her. "Now yank that screen off the pond, and let's have no more of this nonsense. I want my breakfast."

The Cat's mention of the screen and breakfast in almost the same breath started fresh doubts in Mrs. Cary's mind. To what degree had the wire screen been responsible for his keeping his side of the bargain?

"Wouldn't you rather I gave you breakfast first and then

took away the screen?" she asked. "It will take a little time, you know."

"Oh, very well," said The Cat, getting to his feet.

Together they quitted the pool and started for the kitchen door. The fog bank, which had lain offshore all yesterday afternoon had moved in during the night. Now the tops of the trees were lost in mist and, as The Cat trotted into the kitchen ahead of her, Mrs. Cary noticed sparkling beads of moisture caught in his fur.

"What would you like for breakfast?" she asked.

"Just a little warm milk for the present. This fog penetrates to my very bones."

"I should have thought, then, you'd have had the good sense to stay in by the fire last night." She poured some milk into a saucepan and set it on the stove. "I even called to you before I went up to bed."

"Yes, I know. I heard you quite clearly. If you want to know, you sounded ridiculous. Most people do when they call a cat. And no self-respecting cat pays the slightest attention. Imagine anyone answering to the name of 'Kitty'!"

He watched her closely and in a moment said, "That's as warm as I like it."

She turned off the fire, poured the milk into a deep dish which she decided would now be The Cat's dish, and made straight for the coffee pot. While The Cat crouched over his milk, Mrs. Cary went thankfully about the preparation of her own breakfast.

She enjoyed breakfast. She liked all the things there are for breakfast except, possibly, smoked herring. Soon the kitchen was fragrant with the smell of broiling bacon. The

Cat continued indifferent to her as she moved quickly about, popping an egg into boiling water and dropping two slices of bread into the toaster. She drank her fruit juice standing at the stove with one eye on the kitchen clock. The egg would be ruined if it boiled longer than three minutes.

Soon all was ready on the little table under the window. Mrs. Cary seated herself, shook out her napkin, sent a pleased look to the garden outside the window, and settled to her breakfast.

"That man who was here last evening . . ." began The Cat.

Mrs. Cary, having just lifted up the coffee pot, frowned slightly. Since she disliked any conversation before she had taken at least one cup of coffee, The Cat's voice jarred.

"What about him?" she asked sharply.

The Cat took a moment to lick his whiskers before saying, "I don't go much on him."

"Why not?" She bit into a piece of toast.

"Because I don't go much on that Joe he was with."

She chewed thoughtfully before taking another long swallow of coffee.

"Did you know Joe?"

"Certainly I knew him. That's why I slid out when the man who calls himself Mo was leaving. I wanted to get a good look at Joe. He's the same Joe who used to come here now and then to see Mrs. Crow. They were in cahoots, if you ask me."

"I do ask you," she said. "It should have been easy for you to discover that much, since you lived with Mrs. Crow. Or so you said."

"And so I did," returned The Cat. "But they were always extremely cautious about what they said—almost as if they were afraid I *would* understand them." He settled himself close to the linoleum and closed his eyes as an aid to reminiscence. "Matter of fact, Joe and I had no use for each other. He'd always make her throw me out as soon as he came into the house. So I never did find out what it was they were doing. All the same, I had my suspicions," he concluded darkly.

"And what did you suspect?" asked Mrs. Cary. Her tone was indulgent and she was pouring her second cup of coffee.

"Smuggling," said The Cat.

The word so startled Mrs. Cary that she jerked her head around to stare down at him, and the cup ran over.

"Oh, *rats!*" she exclaimed.

Muttering with annoyance, she poured the spilled coffee back into the cup and wiped the saucer with her paper napkin. She looked down again at The Cat. He still sat tight to the linoleum, his tail warming his feet and his eyes sleepy slits. She regarded him thoughtfully.

After all, she told herself, taking a long sip of coffee, he's just a cat.

But she was instantly reminded of The Cat's own definition of himself. "Not *a* cat, but *The* Cat," he had said.

"There's something I'd like to take up with you." She put down the cup and turned slightly to face him.

The Cat raised himself to his haunches and yawned.

She looked into the pink cavern of his mouth. "Are you listening?"

"Every hair a-quiver," he replied with a quick lick at his chest.

"I don't want you ever again to speak out the way you did last night in front of that man," she said firmly.

The Cat raised a paw and wiped his face. "You mean what I said about smugglers?"

"Exactly."

"I had Mo really going there for a minute, didn't I?"

"And made me look like an idiot."

The Cat greeted this with a sneeze that was almost a snicker. "He thought you were off your rocker."

"About this smuggling that Joe and Mrs. Crow were in cahoots on," she went on quickly. "Whatever gave you such a notion?"

"They did."

"But what could they have smuggled?"

The Cat made a pitying sound. "They could have been smuggling anything from aliens to amethysts; from dope to diamonds."

Mrs. Cary returned to her coffee, while a vague memory tugged at her mind. Suddenly she had it. Only last week she had seen something in *The Gull Cry* about smuggling. She hadn't read the article carefully, so now she couldn't remember whether it had actually concerned this particular place or some nearby section of the coast. It must, however, have been of fairly local interest, since *The Gull Cry* was the village weekly.

She set down her coffee cup, rose, and went to her broom closet. It was next to the refrigerator, and The Cat watched her movements closely. But a quick search of the old newspapers neatly stacked there failed to turn up the only two *Gull Crys* she had had time to receive. The whole stack was comprised of *The Big City Daily*, which she got each day through the mail. *The Gull Cry* had obviously been sacrificed to some utilitarian purpose, such as starting the living-room fire.

Oh well, she comforted herself as she returned to her coffee, the item was probably just something out of the past, the safely distant past.

Aloud she said, "It's all too absurdly bizarre. You must remember that we're living in the twentieth century."

To which The Cat replied, "If there's anything more bizarre than the twentieth century, I hope I'm living my ninth life."

Then he rose to his feet, trotted deliberately to the door leading into the living room, and paused expectantly. Mrs. Cary, pretending she hadn't noticed, went on with her coffee. When he had waited for what he considered to be a considerate interval, he turned his head and glared across the kitchen at her.

"Can't you see I want you to open the door?" he cried.

Mrs. Cary sighed and rose. "Sometimes I don't think the goldfish are worth it," she said. "Sometimes I think I'll do away with the pool altogether and make it into a rock garden."

She opened the door just wide enough to let him slip through.

"There are always the birds," he said, letting his tail remain in the opening as he spoke. "I saw a little hummer over the fuchsias this morning that would make a tempting tidbit."

"You're exasperating," declared Mrs. Cary in a tone that caused The Cat to remove his tail. The door shut smartly behind him, and he shuddered his fur all along his back. Then, moving secretly, he approached the sofa, leaped lightly onto it, and slowly settled himself in its soft cushions, nose to tail.

Mrs. Cary returned to the remnants of her breakfast. Smugglers indeed! And yet, suppose The Cat did know what he was talking about? What in heaven's name besides Mrs. Crow's house and Mrs. Crow's cat had she bought? She finished her coffee, set the cup down decisively, and pushed back her chair.

Smugglers or not, there were dishes to be washed and a house to be "pulled together."

The Cat had been dozing the better part of an hour by the time Mrs. Cary had worked her way to the few grains of imaginary dust atop the hospitality table. He opened his eyes at her approach, stretched his front legs, and yawned. Then, as if taking a hint from the dustcloth in her hand, he sat up and began cleaning his shirtfront. Mrs. Cary's eyes flicked from him to her sofa and back again.

"Don't you think you might do that outside?"

The Cat ceased moving his head up and down the front of him to survey her steadily. At last he spoke.

"There's something we might as well understand right now," he began.

Mrs. Cary waited.

"If you knew anything at all about cats, you would know that there is one place in a room which they consider their own and occupy as such. I have chosen this sofa. It is soft and well placed in front the fire. I don't intend to stay anywhere else in this room. It stands to reason, of course, that now and then some of the hairs from my coat will be on the sofa cushions. But since they won't be on any other piece of furniture in here, I think you will have precious little to complain of."

Mrs. Cary turned this over in her mind while The Cat went

to work on his underside. "Very well," she said at last, sighing. "I suppose the vacuum cleaner can get them off."

Quickly The Cat glanced up. "Vacuum cleaner!"

"You don't suppose I'm going to leave those hairs there all day, do you?" she demanded.

Without answering, he jumped off the sofa, hitting the floor with an angry thud. Like a cat who knew where he was going, he headed toward the entry hall. In another moment, there was a flash of light in the shape of a square near the floor. For just an instant it showed, then was gone.

So he didn't stay out all night after all, she thought, heading for the broom closet.

5

THE LETTER

One morning after The Cat and Mrs. Cary had been together for about a week, she was astonished to find a letter lying with *The Big City Daily* in her mailbox. Because she was, as she herself put it, "illetterate," she very seldom heard from anyone except at Christmas time, and then mostly just cards with names on them. But here, today, was a letter!

She picked it up almost gingerly and read the postmark. Lawrence, Kansas. Amy, of course! Only last week Mrs. Cary had written to her sister-in-law announcing her new address and describing in some detail the lovely old house she had bought. Now here, in a mere matter of days, was an answer. And by airmail! This was quite foreign to Mrs. Cary's experience with Amy, whom she considered as "illetterate" as herself. But then, of course, Amy, as the mother of a family, had some excuse.

Mrs. Cary slammed shut the mailbox and turned toward her house.

"Good morning, dear lady. Haven't seen you for a dog's age." The major was marching stalwartly up to the Willoughby mailbox.

"I've been right here," said Mrs. Cary, continuing across the road. A kind of foreboding had begun to settle on her, and she didn't want to be detained. Why had Amy answered so soon?

But the major, as usual, was in a conversational mood.

"Tell me," he began, "how did you make out with that cat? Has he been getting any more fish?"

Mrs. Cary paused in the middle of the road and gave the major a pleasant smile.

"The Cat and I have come to an agreement," she informed him.

The major chuckled dutifully. "You leave the screen on, and he leaves the fish alone," he said, making a gallant effort.

"Not at all." She corrected him. "He leaves the fish alone in exchange for room and board."

The major considered this and gave his mustache a quick swipe. "You're being very foolish," he said soberly.

"Probably," she agreed, "but since Three Corners was once his home, it seemed heartless not to let him stay on here."

"He was Mrs. Crow's cat?"

Mrs. Cary nodded.

"How do you know?"

"Why, The Cat told me so," she replied.

Major Paddleford looked at her for a long moment while Mrs. Cary felt her face grow red. Then he turned toward his mailbox. "Very amusing. Very amusing, I'm sure," he muttered without a trace of amusement.

Mrs. Cary beat a hasty retreat to her garden. But just as

she reached it, The Cat, who had been sitting at the end of the walk all this while, inserted his body between her feet, almost upsetting her. As she flung out her arms to save herself, *The Big City Daily* went one way and Amy's letter went another.

"Are you all right, dear lady?" came a voice from the row of mailboxes.

"Yes, thank you," Mrs. Cary called without looking around and hurriedly reclaimed her mail from among the marguerites.

Her bones and her temper about equally jarred, she would have liked to kick The Cat sauntering unperturbably up the walk ahead of her.

"Am I going to have to step over or around you for the rest of my life?" She flung the words at him fiercely, but The Cat remained unconcerned.

"Unless you outlive me, you will," was all he said, and in a mild tone.

Thankfully she entered the house and began a search for her reading glasses. By the time she found them upstairs on the bedstand she was ready to consign the major, cats, and Kansas to a very dark future.

Seating herself on the edge of the bed, she opened the letter and began to read. She turned the first page, gasped— "Oh, no!"—and took off her glasses. Then she quickly put them on again and continued reading as fast as she could, making little insect noises with her tongue. "Sst; sst!" When she had finished the letter, she jerked off her glasses again and crossed the room to the row of windows which overlooked the road, the cliff, and the spreading sea.

"I can't possibly do it!"

She stuffed the letter back into its envelope and flung it over onto the bed.

"Can't possibly do what?" demanded The Cat, coming into the room.

"I can't have Brad here this summer," Mrs. Cary answered. "That's what I can't."

The Cat leaped lightly onto the bed and sniffed the letter. "Who's Brad?" he asked without much interest.

"He's Amy's oldest boy and my nephew by marriage."

The Cat's interest sharpened visibly. "Suppose you fill me in," he suggested, a hint of anxiety in his voice.

"Like an idiot I wrote to my sister-in-law last week," Mrs. Cary began, "telling her all about Three Corners. I even drew her a plan of the house."

"A bit of the old brag?" observed The Cat.

Mrs. Cary nodded gloomily. "A bit," she admitted.

"So now Amy's found a way to fill that downstairs bedroom. You might have known," he went on pitilessly.

"It's not as cut and dried as all that." Mrs. Cary corrected him, making an honest effort to be fair. "Amy doesn't come right out in so many words. She says that Brad is making a slow recovery from a virus infection, that it's already awfully hot in Kansas, and that the doctor thinks a few weeks at the seaside would work wonders for him. But it's easy to read between the lines. The letter is simply one long hint for me to invite him here."

"Of all the nerve!" exclaimed The Cat.

Those were the very words which had come to Mrs. Cary's own mind on first reading Amy's letter. They had seemed just and reasonable then. But now, as she heard them out of The

Cat's mouth, they took on a different value. She thought of Amy in the old square house on the edge of the campus where her husband was a professor. She could hear the children banging up and down its uncarpeted stairs. She saw Amy in the big old kitchen with its worn linoleum, getting three meals a day for six people and doing it as if it were the greatest fun in the world. Certainly it was the happiest family Mrs. Cary had ever known, though so full of confusion.

She rose from the chair and crossed over to the bed. Again she picked up the letter and slapped it absently against her other palm.

"Not really." She corrected The Cat, speaking thoughtfully. "Really, not at all. Amy has always been very kind to me." She was suddenly remembering all the little thoughtfulnesses Amy had shown during Mr. Cary's last illness. "I suppose she just assumed I would be willing to do as much for her as she for me." This thought shocked her into silence for a moment. When she went on, she spoke more to herself than to The Cat. "I suspect she disliked having to write as she did, but of course her boy's welfare would come before her finer feelings in the matter."

"I have always detested the name of 'Amy,' " observed The Cat irrelevantly. "It's simply 'yam' spelled backwards."

Now, as luck would have it, The Cat in this critical moment had hit upon one of Mrs. Cary's favorite diversions. She adored words and was an avid worker of crossword puzzles. It was her excuse for taking *The Big City Daily*, for which she had no real need. Her kitchen radio gave her the roundup of world news every evening, and *The Gull Cry* accounted for local happenings. Only, *The Big City Daily* had crossword puzzles.

She smiled down at The Cat, grateful for this break in her unhappy thoughts of Amy. She weighed what he had just said and was gleeful to discover him in error.

"That's not so," she declared triumphantly. " 'Amy' isn't 'yam' spelled backwards at all. It's no more 'yam' spelled backwards than it is 'may' spelled backwards. It would be . . . let's see . . . it would be y-m-a, 'yma' spelled backwards."

"Which doesn't make sense," said The Cat, "and neither does Amy. You can't possibly have a boy here."

Mrs. Cary, reluctant to abandon the game so soon, felt annoyed with The Cat.

"Give me one reason why I can't have a boy here," she demanded.

"I hate boys," returned The Cat promptly.

"That's not a good enough reason," said Mrs. Cary.

"A boy simply spells 'chaos,' " he said and added wickedly, "using three letters instead of five."

His teasing went unheeded, for Mrs. Cary was trying desperately to remember what she could about Brad. It proved to be very little, for it was two years since she had last seen him. He had been around ten then, and she knew he must have changed a good deal. How did one entertain a twelve-year-old guest—and a boy, at that? What would they say to each other? She wished she knew something about children. Of course she had once been a child herself, but that was long ago and everything she read seemed to convey the idea that children today were nothing at all the way they used to be. Was this possible?

What could a boy find to do in a sleepy little place like Crow's Harbor? Of course there was the beach. But this boy had no experience of beaches, and the surf here was dangerous. There were crosscurrents and a strong undertow, so he couldn't go bathing. What, then, would he do?

Suddenly panic seized her. She didn't even have TV! For a moment her mind wavered, then set decisively. She wouldn't have it, either, Brad or no Brad.

What would he do with himself all day? She had read once that boredom was in itself a disease. How could Brad, already weakened by virus, combat the boredom of Crow's Harbor? It seemed almost as if he should be protected from the place!

"How do I know he will be happy here?" she asked aloud.

"You don't," The Cat replied, aiding and abetting her doubts. "The kindest thing you could do, and I am sure your only concern is for the boy's own good"—here he eyed her shrewdly—"is to write at once and tell Amy kindly but firmly that the thing just won't do. You simply can't have a boy here."

It was that shrewd cat's glance that really did for Mrs. Cary. Honesty forced her to look deep into her heart and to recognize the truth of what she saw there. The simple truth was, *she didn't want Brad*. She wanted to be left alone to live in peace and order. She intended that all the rest of her days should be spent in reading and walking and housekeeping and gardening. She had figured her finances to a nicety, and with reasonable care she could be certain that her days from now until the grave would be peaceful and predictable.

But alas for all her plans. First a cat and now a boy had thrust themselves in. She sighed and let the letter fall from her hands.

"I may as well write and get it over with," she said, moving toward the desk in the corner.

"If it was me I'd ignore the whole thing," said The Cat. Mrs. Cary ignored his remark.

"I suppose, though, you feel it's your duty to write to this Amy and tell her that you hope Brad will soon be his sturdy little self again."

"I do hope that, of course," said Mrs. Cary, opening a box of stationery.

The Cat rolled onto his side and stretched his hind legs as far as they would go. An almost secret smile of satisfaction curved his neat mouth. He even gave Amy's letter a playful pat where it lay abandoned on the bed.

For a few moments there was only the sound of Mrs. Cary's pen traveling quickly across the paper. Back and forth it went without pause. At last a hint of urgency in the pen's scratching drew The Cat's attention. He looked up in time to see her flip over the paper and continue writing with the same steady purpose. With growing concern he watched until she had finished and put the pen down. Then, as she carefully folded the paper, he heard her mutter, "That will fetch him in a hurry."

The Cat telescoped to attention with stunning swiftness. "Fetch who?"

"Brad, of course. Who else?"

"You're out of your mind."

"Possibly." She reached for an envelope.

The Cat jumped off the bed and landed with an outraged thump. Straight to her chair he went and began rubbing against it, his body turning in ever quicker circles.

"Have you thought of the boy's safety?" he cried. "He's sure to get himself drowned."

"Other children play on the beach and stay alive," she replied calmly.

"He might fall off a rock at high tide—or out of a tree."

Mrs. Cary picked up her pen again and began addressing the envelope.

"The goldfish," The Cat reminded her. "He'll find sticks and poke at 'em to make 'em swim. Poor things. How they do dart about when you poke at 'em. Used to wring my heart."

This drew a grim smile from Mrs. Cary, who thought The Cat was finding a surprising lot for Brad to do.

"And he'll be a cinch to get his feet on the sofa," he continued, eying her closely as he played his trump card. "And he'll mar every table top with the kind of assorted junk boys' pockets are full of," he hurried on, pushing his advantage.

But Mrs. Cary continued to ignore him. She reached for an airmail stamp and stuck it to the letter without so much as a glance at him.

The Cat studied her hopefully for another moment before finally accepting his defeat. Then, stalking determinedly, he went out of the room and descended the stairs on velvet feet. At the bottom he turned and entered the living room and immediately approached one of the gold Victorian chairs. Reaching up both paws, he sharpened his claws thoroughly in the antique velours of its upholstered back. Then, glancing upward, he trotted into the entry and out the cat hole.

6

CRICKET

After leaving the house, The Cat went directly into the back garden, as he did every morning, to admire his reflection mirrored on the shadowy waters of the goldfish pond. He sat very close to the edge and gazed attentively down at himself. No doubt about it, he was filling out. And his coat was almost glossy. Now if he could just do something about those ears . . . A small cone from the tree above dropped into the water with a splash which shattered the reflection and so startled The Cat that he jerked back, spitting. But as soon as the water was smooth again, he returned to his vigil.

Suddenly a flash of gold drew him taut. Out of the dark depths at his feet a form emerged. It fanned up, nibbling, until it lay just under The Cat's reflection. Carefully he reached out a paw. For a moment it hovered threateningly above the unsuspecting fish. Then slowly, reluctantly, it was drawn back, and the golden form floated safely past.

It would be kind to credit this unlikely forbearance to a

twinge of cat conscience, but it would be inaccurate. The
goldfish owed its life to a combination of cold water and warm
milk.

When a truant gust of wind again destroyed The Cat's
mirror, he rose and started for the front garden, which was
more protected. Circling the house, he arrived at the front
walk, where he paused for a cautious look around. This habit
of constant vigilance had kept him alive until this morning.
Within the next few minutes it was to preserve him once
again.

Looking this way and that, The Cat debated with himself.
Should he stretch out under the marguerites for an hour's
snooze, or should he go up the road to where yesterday he
had discovered fresh evidence of a gopher in the neighborhood?

A sudden ear-splitting roar saved him the necessity of making
that decision. The savage sound was close, so close that it
needed no thought at all to dictate The Cat's next move. He
came about from his relaxed crouch and streaked up the
walk toward the house at the best speed he could muster, the
roars sounding hideously close behind him. He reached the
cat hole in the nick of time and popped inside.

Mrs. Cary, still upstairs, also heard the roar, along with the
frantic yells which accompanied it. "Merciful heavens, what's
that?" she cried aloud, at the same time diagnosing the bedlam
as the voices of a dog and a child. Plainly one or the other
was being murdered, and she'd better find out which.

Racing down the stairs, she was in time to see the cat hole
flap shoot inward with such force that it smacked the wall
above it. Simultaneously The Cat burst into the entry hall and
flashed across the living room. He had barely gained the sofa

when again the flap was thrust in. This time a head pushed through and stuck there, transferring the roar from the garden to the house. The old walls vibrated to its swells and rhythms.

"Merciful heavens!" Mrs. Cary cried again as she stared helplessly at the head protruding into her house.

From outside came a command shrieked above the creature's roaring. "Heel, Doc, heel!"

Whatever that command meant, Mrs. Cary could see that it was perfectly futile. The head stayed rammed in the cat hole, the cavern of its mouth as red as a split watermelon and its white fangs gleaming.

Just when it seemed her eardrums could bear no more, she saw the head slowly, grudgingly recede, and the flap fall. Silence, so heavy one could hear it, descended upon Three Corners.

Cautiously Mrs. Cary opened the door a crack. A girl with a big black dog pulled tight against her stood just beyond the porch.

"You can open the door," she called graciously. "I have a leash on him now."

But through the crack Mrs. Cary could see the dog, despite his leash, watching the door with eyes feverishly bright. Now and then he licked his jaws hungrily.

"I'm not sure you can hold him," she said, not widening the crack by so much as a quarter of an inch. "He must weigh a hundred pounds."

"Well, so do I," returned the girl stoutly. "Besides, his collar's a slip chain." She gave the leash a yank. "I could choke him to death if I had to."

Thinking this might be a fine idea, Mrs. Cary opened the

door a little wider. The dog's eyes looked eagerly past her into the house.

"What did you want?" she inquired politely.

"I wondered if this was the haunted house," the girl answered. "You know, the house with the ghost."

Mrs. Cary took a moment to absorb this before saying, "I haven't heard about any ghost." To herself she thought, There can't be a ghost, or Major Paddleford would certainly have reported it.

"Then you haven't seen it." The girl sounded woefully letdown.

Mrs. Cary shook her head, thinking, And with luck I won't. But the child sounded so disappointed she felt almost apologetic toward her. Furthermore her curiosity was piqued. She came out onto the little porch, shutting the door behind her.

"Tell me more," she demanded, smiling.

The girl hesitated for a moment, as if considering where to begin, then took a deep breath and said, "Well, Mr. Santee —you know, he owns Santee's Shanties, the motel where my grandfather and I are staying. Well, Mr. Santee said that when Mrs. Crow was sick—she's the one who used to live in this house, you know." Mrs. Cary nodded. "Well, when Mrs. Crow was sick, Mrs. Santee helped nurse her and one night Mrs. Santee smelled sandalwood. You see, you always smell sandalwood before the ghost walks—"

"Did Mrs. Santee see the ghost?"

"I'm coming to that," said the girl, giving her listener an impatient glance. "Mrs. Santee had heard all about the ghost and the sandalwood and everything. So when she smelled the sandalwood, she knew the ghost *would* walk. Well, she was in bed and so she pulled the covers up over her head and stayed that way, and finally she went to sleep and she never did see the ghost."

"A fine nurse," observed Mrs. Cary dryly. "What's your name?"

"Christine Mobray. But everybody calls me Cricket."

"I'm glad to meet you, Cricket. I'm Mrs. Cary."

Cricket acknowledged the introduction with a smile, then dropped her eyes to the dog in sudden shyness. Her name suited her, Mrs. Cary thought. She was a most attractive girl. Her blond hair hung in a pony-tail, and her eyes, green with brown specks in them, looked straight at you when she spoke. There were brown specks too over the bridge of her nose, and she wore a blue striped cotton jersey pullover with blue denim shorts. Her legs and arms were nicely tanned.

"What kind of dog is that?" asked Mrs. Cary.

"A Doberman," replied Cricket, looking up quickly. "He's really a wonderful dog, but he's young and foolish and he just naturally hates cats. I'm training him to heel."

"Good," said Mrs. Cary, not knowing in the least what Cricket meant but more than ready to support her efforts. Training, any kind of training, was just what this big brute needed. Right now, with his interest in The Cat dwindling, he seemed less formidable. His leash was loose across his back as he sat on his haunches, pressed close against his mistress. Now and then he lifted his head to nudge her arm. Once he took her wrist into his mouth, and Mrs. Cary gasped.

Cricket grinned. "That's just his way of telling me he's tired of waiting. We were headed for the beach, really, but then he saw the cat and started after it before I could grab him. And then when you came to the door, I thought I might as well find out about the ghost."

"I see," said Mrs. Cary.

"Of course, hereafter I'll always have the leash on him when I get near here," she promised.

Silence followed her words. When it threatened to become awkward, a voice from the cat hole broke it.

"Get rid of that kid."

Immediately Doc went into a frenzy, lunging toward the house and roaring mightily. But, true to her word, Cricket was able to manage him. With both hands she hauled him up, choking off his wind and thereby silencing his bark.

"Get rid of that kid," said The Cat again, and again Doc lunged, but silently.

Mrs. Cary decided she had had enough. "It's been very nice meeting you," she said to Cricket. "I'm sorry we haven't more time to chat, but I was just on my way to the village to mail a letter."

"I'll mail it for you," offered the girl. "Doc and I don't really have to go to the beach."

Mrs. Cary hesitated. She hated to seem ungracious, but should she trust this perfect stranger, and a mere child at that, with such an important letter? Cricket couldn't be over ten or eleven—and with a dog distracting her, too.

"It concerns an emergency," she began, "and must be mailed as soon as possible."

"I should think, in that case," said Cricket, "you'd just telephone."

Mrs. Cary stared at her. She had never thought of telephoning! Probably in her whole life she had never placed more than a half-dozen long-distance calls. Why, of course! It was the only thing to do. Brad was ill. Not a day should be lost in getting him here, where he could start to recover. And she wouldn't wait for the rates, either. She would phone right now.

"Come in," said Mrs. Cary.

Together the three entered the house, and The Cat shot out the cat hole.

In less than five minutes Mrs. Cary was talking to Amy. When she hung up, it was decided that Brad would be on his way tomorrow. Amy would wire his flight number and time of arrival at the airport at Kingsmount, four miles from the village.

Mrs. Cary turned from the phone slightly flushed and very pleased with herself. Amy had sounded humbly grateful for Mrs. Cary's offer to keep Brad all summer. For that is what the conversation had resulted in.

"My dear Amy," Mrs. Cary had cried into the phone, "two weeks is no time at all. He should stay a month at least."

"Well-l-l," Amy had replied, drawing out the word, "I don't know about that."

"But he'll be no trouble at all," Mrs. Cary had declared, sweeping Amy's reluctance aside and feeling pleasantly gracious as she made the prediction. "I shall love having him. Why not let him stay until school opens?"

"Well-l-l," Amy had repeated, sounding more dubious this time than she had before.

"I insist," said Mrs. Cary finally with such conviction that Amy could do no more than express her eternal gratitude for such kindness. Her words were so obviously heartfelt that they had brought a glow to Mrs. Cary's face along with the huge sense of well-being already referred to. Why, it was fun to be able to help out now and then! She found herself positively anticipating her nephew's arrival as she went into the living room, where Cricket sat with Doc pulled close against her chair.

"How old is Brad?" the visitor asked. "I couldn't help hearing you," she explained without embarrassment.

"Just about your age, I should think." She stopped and stared at Cricket with mounting delight while Cricket, puzzled, stared back. "Of course!" cried Mrs. Cary. "You and Brad can be friends with each other."

How perfectly everything was turning out! she thought. Here was a companion dropped out of the blue onto her very doorstep to help her entertain Brad. Her problem was ended before it began.

But Cricket dashed her hopes somewhat by saying, "I don't know how long we're going to stay. It will all depend on my grandfather's investigation."

Mrs. Cary remembered now that the child had said they were staying at the motel. "What does your grandfather do?" she asked.

"He works for the government," answered Cricket vaguely, adding, almost as if she wanted to avoid further questions, "My father is in the State Department. He had to go to Paris and my mother went with him. I could have gone too, but I didn't want to leave Doc. Besides, I've been to Paris a dozen times. So Grandy said he'd drive out here and bring Doc if I'd come with him."

"How very interesting," murmured Mrs. Cary who had

never been to Paris and never expected to go now that she had acquired a house and a garden, three goldfish, and a cat —The Cat, she immediately corrected herself.

"At least you'll be here for the next few days," she said. "It will help Brad a lot to have a companion right at the start of his visit."

Cricket offered no comment, and Mrs. Cary went on, thinking out loud, "Let's see now. He will get here sometime early in the evening. And he'll be very tired from the trip. So he'll have dinner and go straight to bed. But I think he'd be glad to see you the next morning. Why don't you come sometime around eleven o'clock? I'll fix a picnic lunch and you can have it on the beach. I'm sure he'd enjoy that."

"Okay," said Cricket without enthusiasm. She rose from her chair, and Doc stood up, eager and expectant. "I guess I'd better be going now."

"But you will come by day after tomorrow?" urged Mrs. Cary. "I'll be counting on you to help me entertain Brad." She had almost said, "To take Brad off my hands."

"Sure," said Cricket. "I'll be here." Mrs. Cary opened the front door, and the girl and her dog stepped onto the porch. "Unless we should have to leave in a hurry," she added over her shoulder. "That happens sometimes in Grandy's business."

Before Mrs. Cary could open her mouth to ask what that business might be, Doc sighted The Cat perched cozily out of reach on the low porch roof. The ensuing clamor made any speech impossible. With waves and smiles Mrs. Cary and her caller took leave of each other. By the time Cricket reached the end of the walk, Doc had resigned himself to the leash

and the futility of mere sound. But by then it was too late to put the question.

Mrs. Cary lingered for a moment outside the house. It had turned out to be a lovely day with a strong smell of salt in the air. A land breeze had blown most of the fog out to sea, where it stood banked darkly on the horizon. Shoreward, the sea was blue under a blue sky, and in every garden round-about birds flashed and sang in joy at the sudden sunshine.

She rather regretted her walk to the village as she stood sniffing the fresh morning. It was just the kind of a day for a good brisk walk. But wait. Now was the time to go to the beach! In the three weeks she had been here, she had not taken the time to do more than walk to the water's edge. Now, this very morning, she would explore along the shore to Wolf's Head Point. She joyously turned back into the house to change into beach shoes and jacket, but before she could reach the coat closet she remembered that this was not, after all, the day for skylarking. Brad was coming tomorrow. She must get the spare room ready. She must check her supply cupboard and phone in her grocery order, and plan her dinner for tomorrow night. It must be a good dinner; first impressions were lasting.

With only a small sigh she climbed the stairs and, from a cupboard beside her bedroom door, began sorting out the spare-room linens.

Out on the roof, The Cat blinked sleepily and settled himself closer onto the warm shingles. A grim smile curled the corners of his mouth.

7

PREPARATIONS

Mrs. Cary woke next morning to sunshine. This was so unusual that she sprang from her bed and pattered out onto the little balcony outside her bedroom door. From here she could look directly down into the living room. She savored its quiet early-morning air with the never-ending pleasure she felt each day on waking. This morning the room seemed unusually charming because a long shaft of sunlight had managed to dodge between the trees of the back garden to enter through the French windows. It laid its long finger right across the room as far as the back of the sofa, where it stopped in a splash of light. Thus it did not disturb the slumbers of The Cat, who was curled in the shadow of the sofa back. Across from the sofa, beyond the front windows, the sea sparkled, a bright and dancing blue.

Mrs. Cary stretched her arms above her head in a kind of ecstasy of contentment, then let them smack down to her sides. This brought The Cat's head up with a jerk. Sighting her above him on the balcony, he at once rose and arched his back.

"Good morning," she called down to him. "Lovely morning, isn't it?"

The Cat, disdaining to reply to a question so banal, simply eyed her appraisingly until she turned back into the bedroom. Then he got off the sofa and started toward the kitchen.

Mrs. Cary ate a hurried breakfast and turned The Cat out into the garden against his will. But a busy day was in the offing, and she didn't want any interruptions of any kind, and The Cat was, by his very nature, an interrupter. Brad was arriving this evening. Much remained to be done.

For one thing, the refrigerator must be thoroughly cleaned of left-overs. She had no idea what kind of food Brad would prefer, or what he might be required to eat, and there must be plenty of room when it would be needed. This meant that bowls and jars and little plastic dishes of all sizes must be dumped and put to soak. When all had been accomplished, she went out with the big paper bag to the garbage can.

The garbage can concealed itself discreetly behind a lattice overgrown with morning-glory vines. As a matter of fact, the lattice had proved quite insufficient for their lofty ambitions. So, hitching onto a gutter pipe, they had hoisted themselves up the side of the old building almost to Mrs. Cary's bedroom window.

Having disposed of the bag and put the lid back firmly, Mrs. Cary smiled up at the morning glories with real affection. They made taking out the garbage almost a pleasure, and this morning in the sunshine they brought to her mind a song she had learned a million years ago when she was in the first grade. How did it go, exactly? Ah, now she had it! Tentatively, Mrs. Cary began to sing:

"Oh, the morning-glory bells
　Are swinging, ringing,
　Swinging, ringing,
　Under my casement, high."

Her voice gained confidence as the little song came flooding back:

"Purple bells and white ones,
　Pinkly blushing bright ones,
　Pealing forth their music
　To the morning sky."

"Somebody's happy this morning," boomed a voice over the back fence.

Mrs. Cary jumped and, turning, discovered Major Paddleford on the other side of the fence, plump in the middle of Mrs. Kane's rose garden. Mrs. Kane was smiling over his shoulder at her eccentric neighbor.

"It's a morning to make anyone sing," said Mrs. Cary defensively.

"And such an appropriate song," returned the major.

Considerably flustered, Mrs. Cary sought desperately for words to change the conversation. "My nephew's arriving this evening," she announced with evident pleasure.

"Really?" said Mrs. Kane politely. The major took a step closer to the fence.

"Yes." Mrs. Cary rattled on, wondering why she couldn't

just nod and proceed up the walk and into the kitchen as she longed to do. "He's been very ill and is coming here to recuperate."

"You don't say," said the major, all attention.

"It'll be nice for you to have someone else in the house for a change," said Mrs. Kane, who also lived alone.

"Oh yes," returned Mrs. Cary glibly. "I'm looking forward to having Brad. I just hope he won't be too bored here. I know so little about children."

"You mean he's just a child?" demanded the major.

Mrs. Cary nodded. "Around twelve, I'd say."

The major gave his mustache a swipe and looked grave. "Boys can be a problem," he said, "especially nowadays. Twelve," he muttered, shaking his head. "Almost a teen-ager."

Mrs. Cary glanced from one pitying face to the other and felt her gay spirits of a moment before begin to flag.

"Tell you what," said the major, "if he starts to get out of hand, you let me know. Nothing like a man at a time like that, you know." He gave a little apologetic cough. "I don't need to remind you that I've had no small amount of ex- perience in discipline."

Mrs. Cary stared back at him in amazement. How dared this near-stranger offer to interfere in a matter involving her- self and a member of her own family!

"Thank you, Major," she said without a trace of gratitude, "but I'm sure Brad will be no problem."

"A firm hand, dear lady. Remember, a firm hand."

Now Mrs. Cary did nod, first to Mrs. Kane, who looked highly approving of the major, and then to the major, whose

blue eyes under their beetling white brows glinted with remembered firmness.

"I'll remember," she said and returned to her kitchen.

For the next several hours it clattered with activity. As
she worked, Mrs. Cary's irritation with the major was forgotten.
Her spirits rose again. She enjoyed cooking and found it
pleasant to be preparing a real dinner for someone besides
herself. A stack of pots and pans rose steadily within the
sink, while a rich blend of earth's finest odors wreathed the
kitchen. The grocer's boy, dropping in with the weekly order,
much of it comprising tonight's dinner, pulled the good smells
deep into his lungs and grinned appreciatively at the cake
layers cooling on the table.

"If I had it iced, I'd give you some," said Mrs. Cary, bustling
to make room for the groceries.

"I'll take a rain check," said the grocer's boy and went
crashing out of the kitchen and back to his truck.

Shortly thereafter, The Cat announced himself at the back
door. Mrs. Cary, on her way to the refrigerator, detoured to
let him in.

"Just saw the grocery truck drive away," he said. "Any fresh
fish?"

"You know perfectly well it's hours before dinner."

"Then why all this stir and bustle?"

"Didn't you know that Brad is coming tonight?"

"Clairvoyance is not one of my achievements," confessed
The Cat, without regret, then added, "Amy didn't lose any
time, did she?" He leaped onto a chair and surveyed the
kitchen with great disgust. "You'd think he was quintuplets."

Mrs. Cary swung around to the refrigerator again, and The

Cat lifted his head for a hasty look into its interior.

"He won't eat half the stuff you're fixing."

"How do you know?" she demanded over the noise of the eggbeater.

"How do I know? Because for the past several summers I have watched dozens of kids on the beach. All they eat is hamburgers, hot dogs, and ice cream, washing it down with soda pop." His whiskers curled with loathing at the whole idea.

"That's at the beach," returned Mrs. Cary confidently. "It's different when they're home."

"Want to bet?" asked The Cat.

Mrs. Cary smoothed her knife over the top layer of the cake, giving it a final flourish. "Do you mean to tell me that Brad won't want this cake?"

"Depends on how much frosting you put on it." He dropped a critical eye to her handiwork. "Take my advice, dear lady, as the major says, and cover those sides. There's a lot of cake showing."

Mrs. Cary looked worriedly into the bowl. "I don't think there's enough to cover the sides."

The Cat moved the last inch of his tail ever so slightly. "Too bad," he said. "What's for dinner?"

"Ham," said Mrs. Cary, trying to make the frosting reach all the way around. A lot of cake showed through.

"Ham!" said The Cat. "You're kidding."

"Indeed I'm not. Nothing's better."

"I agree," said The Cat grimly.

"And if dinner has to wait," went on Mrs. Cary, "nothing waits better. I can have it baked before I leave for the airport and glaze it when we get back. And it's dependable. Everybody likes ham."

"I don't," declared The Cat.

A shadow of doubt crossed Mrs. Cary's face. Hurriedly she unwrapped the ham and eyed it with suspicion. Near it lay another package of meat. This was the ground round she had ordered "just in case." But you couldn't give your nephew hamburgers for his first dinner in your house. What would Amy think? But suppose The Cat was right? Suppose Brad really didn't like ham? She looked from the ham to The Cat and back again and sighed. Oh dear, it was all so annoying. Here she had been positively enjoying a chance to get dinner for someone again, and then The Cat had to come squalling around to fill her mind with doubt and indecision! It was most upsetting. Besides, thanks to The Cat, the cake looked a perfect mess. She'd have to make some more frosting, that's all there was to it.

Again the tip of The Cat's tail moved. "You still haven't answered my first question," he reminded her.

She looked at him with exasperation. "What question? You ask so many I can't keep up with them."

"Any fresh fish? Besides those in the pond, of course."

Mrs. Cary sighed again, heavily this time, and opened the refrigerator. "Well, maybe it would be wise to feed you now and get it over with. Then I don't want another squeak out of you until tomorrow's breakfast."

The Cat received this in haughty silence. He kept his chair until she had placed his dish on the floor. Then he rose, arched his back, thudded onto the linoleum and moved with great dignity toward his early supper.

By the time he had finished with it, Mrs. Cary had stirred up some fresh frosting and was generously covering the cake's sides. The Cat leaped again onto the chair and watched her lazily.

"What have you been doing with yourself today?" she asked pleasantly. The cake looked simply delicious now, and she was almost grateful for The Cat's timely interference.

"I've been about my business," replied The Cat.

"Which is . . . ?" prompted Mrs. Cary.

"My business." The Cat purred.

"Dear me, we are getting secretive." Mrs. Cary began licking the frosting knife and took a step back to admire the cake. Then she glanced at the clock. There was still plenty of time for fixing the ham, straightening up the kitchen, setting the table, and getting herself ready to leave for the airport. Around noon a telegram had come from Amy informing her of Brad's flight number and time of arrival.

The Cat waited until she had cleared the sink and started to wash up before jumping down from his chair and announcing his desire to be let out. He stood now close to the kitchen door, pressing his side against it and yelling his need above the rattle of the pots and pans.

Mrs. Cary lifted her hands from the dishwater, slid the suds off them, and went to obey The Cat's summons, her mouth set.

"Sometimes, I wonder," she muttered, deliberately withholding her eyes from the cake, which rested in frosted splendor on the kitchen table.

8

BRAD

The bus to Kingsmount creaked and hissed its way over the hill and through the town and up to the airport bus stop. It was just six o'clock, and Brad's plane was due to land in fifteen minutes. Mrs. Cary went inside and sat down. Slowly the minutes crept past, while her heart began to beat at an increased tempo. A kind of dreadful excitement was building up in her. She hadn't felt anything like it since, as a little girl at school, she awaited her turn to recite. Was Brad feeling like this too? She wondered.

She glanced at the clock on the wall across the small lobby. The plane should be arriving. Just then a voice spoke out of the wall above Mrs. Cary's head.

"United Airlines' northbound flight number Three-fifty-six will arrive at Kingsmount at six forty-five." There it was. No explanations; no apologies. Just thirty more minutes to wait. Well, no amount of explanations or apologies could shorten the time by so much as a split second. Mrs. Cary sighed, fidgeted, then rose and went out to the steps facing the field, where the wind began to pull her hair apart. How wise she had been to have a ham! She could think of her waiting dinner with an easy mind. Everything was ready. She smiled, remembering how pretty the table looked. Brad would know at once that his arrival had been carefully planned for.

She poked at her hair and looked interestedly about her. It was a pleasant little airport, hemmed in by oak-grown hills, low and rolling. They opened toward the town of Kingsmount to reveal the bay, flat and blue under the westering sun. Only comparatively small planes landed here, shuttling passengers back and forth between the big cities where the jets landed. Little more than three weeks ago she had flown into this very place to take up her abode at Three Corners. The thought turned her to where in the distance a gray ribbon of concrete climbed a hill off to her left, and she knew this was the highway to Crow's Harbor, four miles away. Now here she was, awaiting her first guest with a mounting excitement in which there was a great deal more dread than pleasure. If only she knew more about children, and especially boys! Why couldn't it have been one of Amy's two girls?

She thought of Cricket. Would that girl show up tomorrow? She had promised, and she looked a dependable sort of child. Still, she had said something about the possibility of leaving suddenly. Something to do with her grandfather's work. What was it she had said about that?

A sudden throbbing in the skies overhead put a stop to Mrs. Cary's speculations about Cricket. Again a voice droned out of the walls. Flight 356 was landing! In a matter of minutes, a few short minutes, she and Brad would be face to face!

She descended the steps to stand at the low fence edging the field. She watched the plane circle the hills and swing into the east. It banked and came in, landing in a rush and a roar. Steadily it taxied up to the fence, turned sharply and stopped. Flight 356 had arrived.

Mrs. Cary watched tensely as the passengers began to emerge. One by one they came down the steps, men with brief cases, men with golf bags, women with babies, women without babies, soldiers with little leather boxes dangling by straps. Would Brad never appear? Just when she was beginning to wonder if he had missed his connection with the local plane, out he came. At least she thought it must be he, since he seemed to be the only boy aboard. As he came closer to her, she could detect a look of Amy about him. Yes, it was Brad all right. He came slowly toward the fence, almost as if he were putting off reaching it. Mrs. Cary waved a shy little wave at him, but if Brad saw it he gave no indication that he had.

At last he was through the gate and they were shaking hands.

"Welcome to Crow's Harbor!" cried Mrs. Cary and let go of Brad's hand, which had lain limply in her own. "Was the trip very tiring?"

He looked about him, unsmiling. "I thought this was Kingsmount," he said, ignoring her question.

"Well, yes, I suppose it is," said Mrs. Cary. "But we'll only be here long enough to claim your baggage. Crow's Harbor is where you're really going to stay."

They moved off toward the baggage counter at the other end of the fence. "How is everybody at home?" demanded Mrs.

Cary, determined to bridge with chatter this awkward moment of their meeting. Brad seemed abnormally unresponsive, but then, of course, he had been very ill and was still far from well. "Nobody else has caught the virus, I hope?"

"They're okay," he replied, his eyes on the path. Then he lifted his head and added, a little defiantly, she thought, "Mom and Dad said to be sure and thank you for inviting me."

"You're very welcome," returned Mrs. Cary, realizing as she dutifully spoke the words that Brad had not actually thanked her at all.

By this time they had reached the baggage counter and Brad stepped forward to present his check. As he stood waiting while the porter checked the number, Mrs. Cary took careful note of her visitor.

He wasn't exactly the kind of boy that stands out in a crowd. But what boy ever does? she promptly asked herself. His dark hair had been recently plastered down, so he had tendencies toward neatness. But he hadn't succeeded with the hair toward the back of his head, which stood up two inches above the rest of his scalp, a little like an Indian feather. He had had a recent haircut. His ears stood out from the sides of his head as if they were trying to hear everything. She couldn't quite remember his eyes, having only had a quick glimpse into them as he came up to the gate. But she thought they were dark, like his hair. He was wearing tan sneakers and brown slacks and a brown windbreaker that looked fleece-lined. Just the thing for the beach, she decided.

The porter finally grabbed hold of a large metal suitcase and with obvious effort swung it up onto the counter.

"What you got in here, son?" he demanded good-naturedly. "Gold bricks?"

"Not exactly," said Brad as he took possession of the suitcase and with difficulty lowered it to the ground.

Mrs. Cary hurried forward. "That's the biggest suitcase I ever saw," she declared. "You can't carry it by yourself."

Brad had already made that discovery and was standing beside the suitcase, looking helplessly around him. Mrs. Cary took hold of the handle and tried to lift it.

"What in heavens name *do* you have in this?" she demanded irritably.

"Books," returned Brad.

She stared at him. "*Books?*"

"Yes, books," he stated, looking at her very directly. His eyes were dark, and right now openly defiant.

"Did you suppose you were going to darkest Africa? Didn't your mother tell you that I have books? A lot of books?"

"About space science?" Brad's voice was politely inquiring.

"Well, no," admitted Mrs. Cary, then added spunkily, "but the Bookmobile will bring you anything you want."

"That would take a week or two, if they had them," said Brad. "I need these books now." He looked back at the plane; preparations for its departure were in progress. "I'm going to be an astronaut."

Mrs. Cary had been looking over her shoulder, hoping to catch the porter's eye when he had finished with distributing the luggage. But Brad's startling announcement swung her gaze back to him.

She found it difficult to see in the sick and sullen boy wistfully looking after the plane that had landed him here, two

thousand miles from home, the sturdy qualities that inter-
stellar travel demanded of its pioneers. There was something
incongruous, too, in his confident hope that these books he
was too weak to lift would help him toward his goal.

Then her eyes softened. Incongruous, all right, and abso-
lutely wonderful. This is the way Columbus must have felt
when, a poor boy in Genoa, he had sat on those piers and
gazed wistfully across the waters to his own private dreamland.
Why shouldn't Brad hitch his wagon to a star? He had the
courage, that was plain. For he had come here against his will.
That also was plain. All the time that she had not been wanting
him, he had not wanted to come. Yet here he was, with a
suitcase of books beside him. Unbidden and with wry amusement, The Cat's words of warning came into her mind. "A
boy spells 'chaos.' "

Certainly not this boy. All her fears had been groundless.
Brad wouldn't fall out of trees or off cliffs or into fishponds.
Why, he wouldn't even want to look at TV if she possessed
a set! A boy who lugged a hundred pounds of books all the
way from Kansas would not be likely to risk spoiling his mind
with trashy entertainment. Brad had turned out to be exactly
the kind of boy she hadn't even dared hope for. What a pleasure it would be to tell The Cat how wrong he had been!
Anticipating the moment, she gave a little chuckle of satisfaction.

Instantly Brad jerked his head around. "What's so funny?"
he demanded. "Don't you believe I can be an astronaut?"

Mrs. Cary shook her head quickly and laid an impulsive
hand on his shoulder. "I wasn't laughing at that, Brad, believe me. Of course you can become an astronaut, or anything

else you care to set your mind to." His eyes remained suspicious, however, and she felt further explanation necessary. "I was just remembering something The Cat said."

He studied her for a moment. "What do you mean 'the cat said.' Who's the cat?"

"Why, he's a cat that came to my house about a week ago."

"Just a plain ordinary cat?"

"Well, hardly ordinary," said Mrs. Cary. "He has a definite personality and a considerable fund of practical knowledge." She hesitated for a moment, as if trying to make up her mind about something. At last she went on. "You see, The Cat doesn't seem to care much for boys. He says they spell 'chaos.' I think it's only fair to tell you right now that The Cat didn't want you at Three Corners at all."

Brad accepted this information without visible shock. For a moment he looked down the field after the departing plane, as if he too were making up his mind about something. Then he said, "Well, you can tell him for me that it's mutual. I didn't want to come here, either."

"You've rather given me that impression," said Mrs. Cary quietly.

"Mom said you were a very particular housekeeper."

"Did she?" replied Mrs. Cary. "Is that why you didn't want to come?"

"That's one reason. You see, I'm not used to it."

"I know," said Mrs. Cary dryly. "But you will have your own room and you can clutter it to your heart's content. And we aren't going to worry too much about the rest of the house. You're here to get well, and that's all that is going to be important to me while you *are* here."

Brad listened with lowered head and with his lips pressed tightly together. A small silence followed her words, and then he looked up into her eyes.

"Do you think maybe the cat might change his mind about wanting me to come? I like cats, you know."

Mrs. Cary's face lighted with sudden joy. "I have an idea, knowing The Cat the way I do, that somehow already he's got a new feeling about you. He's probably sitting on the front walk right now, ready to greet you with open arms."

"I didn't know you had a cat," said Brad. "It makes a difference. I really like cats."

"I thought boys liked dogs," said Mrs. Cary.

"Some of 'em do," replied Brad. "I happen to like cats."

Mrs. Cary shook her head, bewildered. "I never will understand children," she confessed.

"I'm almost thirteen," Brad corrected her.

"Really?" said Mrs. Cary, throwing him an anxious look. "I don't understand teen-agers either."

"That figures," declared Brad. "Neither do Dad and Mom."

"But they *must*," insisted Mrs. Cary. "They're parents!"

"So what?" asked Brad with the air of one who doesn't expect an answer.

The porter was now having his problems with a passenger whose luggage had failed to arrive.

Mrs. Cary stooped toward the suitcase. "Come on, Brad. I think if we tackle this together we can manage it."

And together they did.

9

TUCKING IN THE NEIGHBORHOOD

Although they could have managed to get the suitcase on the bus, they could never have carried it from the bus stop to Three Corners. So they took a taxi from the airport.

As it drew up in front of the old house, Mrs. Cary looked quickly toward the porch, hoping the find The Cat waiting. But of course he wasn't, and she felt unreasonable annoyance. But then, if she had learned one thing about The Cat, it was that he never did the hoped-for.

The taxi driver carried the suitcase to the door and deposited it with a clang on the flagstone floor of the porch.

Mrs. Cary reached into her purse for the fare and the tip and called her thanks to the driver as he ran back to his car. She took the key from under the mat, inserted it into the lock, and flung the door open.

"Welcome to Three Corners," she said, and Brad walked in.

He stood for a moment, looking from the entry down the long living room with its paneled walls, its rows of books, its fieldstone fireplace, and the dining table set in the alcove next to the kitchen.

"It's nice," he said and, turning toward her, smiled for the first time. "It's old, like our house."

"Why, I suppose it is," said his aunt. "In fact, I'll bet it's even older than your house—much older." She opened the door into the spare bedroom. "This is yours," she told him, "strictly yours."

Brad followed her inside and looked carefully around.

"This window," said Mrs. Cary, explaining needlessly, "looks out to sea, and this one right out onto the front garden."

Brad walked to the seaward window. "I've never seen the ocean before. Mind if I go down there?" he motioned toward the beach.

"Why, of course not," said Mrs. Cary. "I expect you'll spend most of your time on the beach."

"I mean right now," said Brad.

Mrs. Cary hesitated. Wasn't this boy too weary for further exertion? Shouldn't he rest while she got dinner ready? Wouldn't it be better if he used his energy to unpack his bag?

"I suppose I can trust your good sense," said Mrs. Cary. "You won't overtire yourself, will you? I suppose it would feel good to stretch your legs a bit after that long ride." Inspiration suddenly wrapped her round. "When you come in, you can phone your mother and tell her all about it."

Brad sent her a quick, surprised smile as he turned from the window.

"Thanks, Aunt Cary," he said and was out the door and away.

He descended the cliff and walked slowly across the sand toward the water. The roar of the breakers filled his ears with a sound entirely new. Off on the rim of the world a line of brightness lay above the slate-blue sea, marking the spot where the sun had just been swallowed. At a little distance from the shoreline he stopped to let his eyes fill themselves with this first real sight of the sea. For all its strangeness, there was something familiar about it. He studied the great swells moving constantly shoreward in unending and unvarying rhythms. Suddenly he had it. The ocean was not unlike a Kansas wheatfield under the wind. It seemed alive in the same remote way. And he knew that, from this moment, whenever he looked upon a wheatfield with the wind running across it, he would think of it as a kind of inland sea.

A little beyond his feet a group of gulls stood flat-footedly contemplating the moving waters. Brad clapped his hands, and the birds flew up, circling in conflicting spirals. The gray of their wings merged with the graying sky, but the whiteness of their breasts gleamed brightly in that light from the sunken sun.

He walked toward the water, with the gulls still flying and calling above him. To the very edge of the land he went and stood wondering as the tireless tide came flowing up the beach, whitening the sands as it fanned out, hissing gently.

Off to his left, Wolf's Head Point loomed darkly against the sky. Brad studied it, amused to find in its jagged outline the head of an animal, perhaps a dog. To his right, another arm of land reached out to form Crow's Harbor.

He turned to look behind him. Three Corners had disappeared, swallowed up in its trees and the gathering dusk. But farther east the hills rose beneath a God's handful of stars. There was no wind, and a kind of suspense lay upon the earth. Brad could feel it, and with the feeling his heart began to beat a little faster. As he watched the line of hills a radiance appeared behind them. Gradually a thin edge of luminous white began to grow, until at last the moon hung full and clear in the night sky, and all the valley swam in silver light. He thought he had never seen the world so beautiful before.

"Good evening, young man!"

Brad, startled, turned quickly to find a tall, heavy-set man standing near him. The man carried a walking-stick and had a small white mustache.

"Paddleford is the name. Major Paddleford," said the man, putting out his hand.

Brad took the hand shyly. "I'm Brad Willets." He nodded in the general direction of Three Corners. "Mrs. Cary is my aunt."

"I suspected as much," declared the major. "I know she's been looking forward to your visit. Indeed, she told me so."

Brad looked thoughtful at these words. They certainly didn't square with the way the cat had felt. But then, perhaps there were many ways of "looking forward" to something.

"Are you a friend of Aunt Cary's?"

The major gave his mustache a quick swipe. "Well, let's say an acquaintance. I'm a neighbor, you might say, who may in time become a friend. Your aunt hasn't lived here very long, you know."

"Yes, I know," said Brad.

"And where is your home?" asked the major.

"Kansas. Lawrence, Kansas. My father's a professor in the university there."

"Science?" hazarded the major.

"Yes," said Brad. "Geology."

"And is your aunt from Lawrence, Kansas, too?"

"No. She's from Cleveland."

"Ah," said the major. Now he knew. Suddenly his air grew brisk and he swung his cane. "It's my habit," he declared to the boy, "to tuck in the neighborhood for the night. I wonder if you would care to join me?"

Mystified, Brad murmured a dubious "Okay," and the major began leading him away from the shoreline and toward the cliff. They puffed up to the road together, where the major struck out sturdily, swinging his stick as he went. Three Corners was nowhere in sight, and Brad guessed that he was turned around. A twinge of uneasiness seized him and quickly went. Aunt Cary was counting on his good sense. It didn't seem that he had been gone long, and he wasn't tired. Besides, this old man wouldn't walk very far. He'd been so friendly, it didn't seem polite not to go along with him.

They had gone more than a half-mile and were almost to the village proper when Brad suddenly realized that he could go no farther. He said as much to the major, who looked shocked.

"Tired? So soon?" he demanded. "Boys were different in my day. You've got to have stamina to make your way in the world, young man."

"Yes, I know," agreed Brad miserably. How he hated to

admit his illness! "Most of the time I have just oodles of stamina. But I've had some kind of virus. That's the reason I'm here."

The major was instantly all kindly concern. "Of course, my dear boy. I remember now. Your aunt mentioned the fact that you had been ill. How thoughtless of me." He helped Brad seat himself on the edge of the road. "How very thoughtless of me," he repeated. He scowled down worriedly at Brad, touched his mustache, and said in a voice determinedly cheerful, "But you'll soon be yourself again. Nothing like the sea winds to put vigor into you."

Brad said nothing to this, and the major began looking helplessly about, as if he expected the night to offer some assistance.

Suddenly two headlights appeared, approaching slowly.

"Ha," said the major and stepped right into the middle of the road. He held up his hand with the authority of a whole squad of police and waited for the car to stop.

"I wonder if you could give us a lift for a couple of blocks or so," he inquired of the two men inside the car.

"Why, I guess so," came the answer. "Anything wrong?"

"Nothing serious," returned the major. "My young companion here seems to have turned his ankle. Painful, of course, but nothing serious."

"Sure. Get in."

Brad let the major help him into the back seat, grateful for the kindly falsehood that had saved his pride. At least these strangers needn't know that he was an invalid.

"Where to?" asked the driver.

"A place called Three Corners," replied the major, eying

the driver closely. "You turn right at the next corner, and it's down the street—"

"I know where it is," said the driver, starting the car.

The major settled back against the seat and studied the two in front of him. At last he cleared his throat.

"Aren't you the gentlemen who called at Mrs. Cary's a few nights ago?" he asked.

The driver glanced up into the rear-view mirror as if from force of habit, because it was now too dark to see anyone in the back seat. But the light from the instrument panel made the two on the front seat clearly visible.

"What of it?" demanded the driver rudely.

"Why, nothing at all, of course," said the major hastily. "I just make it a point never to forget a face, and then when you said you knew where Three Corners was I thought I placed you."

The man beside the driver turned and looked at Brad. "Do you live with Mrs. Cary?" he asked.

"I'm visiting her," said Brad. "I just got here a little while ago."

"I see," said the man, turning again to face the front. Suddenly he looked around again. "Then you must be Brad. Cricket told me about you."

"Cricket?" said Brad.

The man chuckled. "Of course you wouldn't have had time to find out about her. She's my granddaughter, and she and Mrs. Cary have sort of put their heads together over you. I believe Cricket's due to call on you tomorrow."

"Yeah?" said Brad without enthusiasm. Didn't Aunt Cary know any boys?

They came to the Willoughby garden. "You can drop me off here," said the major. He turned to Brad. "Three Corners is just down at the end of the street. I'll look in on you tomorrow, old chap. Take care of that ankle." He got down from the car heavily, and they drew away.

"Need any help?" asked Cricket's grandfather when they were stopped in front of Three Corners.

"No, thanks," said Brad. "I'm okay. Thanks for the ride."

"Glad we came along," said Mr. Mobray.

Brad waited until the car had pulled away, and then he turned to go up the walk. He had taken two steps when suddenly he stopped. Facing him, and looking ghostly in the moonlight, was a large white-chested cat. Like a ghost, he seemed poised for instant take-off. This must be the cat his aunt had referred to at the airport, Brad thought, the cat who hadn't wanted him here.

For fully fifteen seconds the two faced each other. Then slowly Brad dropped to one knee, while The Cat regarded him steadily. Carefully Brad extended a hand, which The Cat eyed warily. Knowledgeable in the ways of cats, the boy waited patiently, hand extended. Then it happened, as Brad knew it would happen. The Cat lowered himself to the walk and, still facing the boy, rolled over abjectly. Brad got to his feet and approached The Cat, one slow step at a time. At last he crouched again and, reaching out, just barely touched The Cat's side. The Cat rolled again, presenting his other side. Brad shuffled closer and began to scratch behind The Cat's ears. The Cat permitted this only briefly before whipping himself into an upright position. When Brad rose too, The Cat lifted up his face to him and meowed once, softly. At this,

Brad stooped and swept The Cat into his arms, where The Cat lay almost contentedly for a moment. But his tail, beating against the boy's knees, proclaimed the fact that he had no intention of staying long. When he did make efforts to escape, Brad relaxed his hold at once, and The Cat bounded away into the night.

"Where have you been?" called Mrs. Cary cheerfully as Brad entered the house. "I was just beginning to get worried.'

A fire was burning on the hearth; soft lamplight glowed in spots around the room, making its corners shadowy. Over on the dining table candles held small tongues of flame aloft above a platter of ham and all the good things to go with it.

"I ran into some people you know," said Brad.

"Oh?" said Mrs. Cary. "Who?"

"There was a major and Cricket's grandfather and—"

"Cricket's *grandfather?*"

"Why, yes," said Brad. "As a matter of fact, he brought me home."

"We'll call your mother first, and after you have talked to her I want to hear all," declared Mrs. Cary, moving toward the phone.

In minutes Brad was saying, "Hi, Mom," and Mrs. Cary was off in the kitchen, where she could under no circumstances hear another word. After a while, quite a long while, a while so long that she was beginning to remind herself that she would have to compensate in her budget somehow for this day's extravagances, the taxi ride and the long-distance call, Brad pushed open the kitchen door.

"And how are things at home?" asked Mrs. Cary.

"They're okay," said Brad in a voice not quite his own.

After a moment he added, "I wasn't talking all that time."

"Well, you very well could have been for all I care," returned Mrs. Cary stoutly, suddenly realizing what it must be like to be twelve and two thousand miles from home and homesick. Sympathy made her reckless, and she added, "I think it might be a good idea to call your mother every week and give her a report. Don't you?" The budget could go hang. Before Brad could frame an answer, she was rattling on, almost as if she were trying to prevent his talking. "Now let's have dinner," she said at last. She whisked off her apron and flung it over the back of one of the kitchen chairs. "I want to hear all about your running into Major Paddleford and Cricket's grandfather—especially Cricket's grandfather."

Brad seated his aunt and then took his own place at the table. And thanks to the major's tucking in of the neighborhood, talk flowed easily back and forth between the candlesticks.

It turned out that Brad didn't like sweet potatoes, so ate his ham in sandwiches. He ate three, washed down with an equal number of glasses of milk. When at last Mrs. Cary brought in the cake, his face lighted for the first time since his arrival.

"Golly, Aunt Cary, that's a super cake and just the way I like it—lots of frosting."

"The Cat said you'd want lots of frosting," she said in a matter-of-fact voice. "I've never cooked for a boy before, but he seemed to know all about it."

Brad looked up from his plate and grinned at his aunt. "I saw the cat when I was coming up the walk," he informed her.

Mrs. Cary nodded. "I thought you might. I fed him early. What did you think of him?"

Brad took a swallow of milk and licked away the mustache. "He's a real good cat. Sensible."

Mrs. Cary laid down her fork, impressed. "Now how in the world can you tell a sensible cat from one that isn't?"

Brad shrugged. "I dunno. Just a feeling you get about 'em, I guess. Either they meet you halfway, or they don't. Your cat met me halfway. So—he's sensible!"

"Yes," agreed Mrs. Cary thoughtfully, "he does meet one halfway."

"What's his name?" asked Brad.

"He doesn't have a name. He told me just to call him The Cat, capital T, capital C. Said it suited him."

Brad smiled, then nodded soberly. "He's right. It does suit him."

When dinner was done and the candles snuffed, Brad wanted to help carry out the dishes, but Mrs. Cary wouldn't hear of it.

"When you've had a chance to rest up, I'll find all sorts of things for you to do. Meanwhile, the kitchen end of it is mine. So you scoot along and hang up your clothes and hop into bed. I'll come in to say good night when I get through here."

So Brad scooted along, and Mrs. Cary went about her business, leaving her guest to his own resources.

Some time later, with the kitchen clock pointing to nine, she put the light out and entered the living room. She stood for a moment, listening, but could hear no sounds from the guest room. Moving on tiptoe, she went into the entry. No light was coming through Brad's door, which stood ajar.

Hesitating a moment, she pushed it gently wider and went into the room. Brad was asleep all right; she could hear his light snoring.

Moonlight was streaming in through the garden window. A path of it lay across the bed, and in its light Mrs. Cary saw something cuddled in the sleeping boy's arms. At first she couldn't quite make it out and wondered if that heavy suitcase had contained, along with his books and clothes, some well-loved toy from his little boyhood.

As she watched, the "toy" moved the tip of its tail ever so slightly, and Mrs. Cary stifled a gasp. The Cat! She bent over the bed. Brad lay with a smile on his closed lips. It hadn't been his snoring after all, but The Cat's loud purring she had heard! Now he lifted his head slightly, and his eyes, catching the moonlight, blazed up at her. The purring stopped, and she heard him say in a voice just barely above a purr, "Mind your own business."

Very carefully Mrs. Cary backed from the room, remembering to leave the door a little ajar.

10

ALTERCATIONS

Mrs. Cary had finished her first cup of coffee when Brad came into the kitchen next morning. He was in pajamas and bathrobe and looked tousled and sleepy.

"Morning," he said, yawning hugely.

"Good morning," returned Mrs. Cary. "How did you sleep?"

"Fine, thanks."

"Where's your sleeping partner?"

Brad grinned. "He left sometime before daylight, I think. How did you know he was sleeping with me?"

"I checked on you after I had finished with the dishes, and there he was." She got up and started toward the refrigerator. "By the way, you went to sleep so quickly you couldn't have had time to unpack your suitcase."

"No," said Brad. "All at once I just felt too pooped to bother with it. Besides, I hate to unpack. I thought maybe you'd help me."

"Of course I will," said Mrs. Cary.

She put two plates down on the table under the window and arranged the silver beside them.

"I guess I'd better go get my clothes on."

"Not this morning, Brad. You're a privileged person this morning. Just sit down there and drink your orange juice and talk to me," said his aunt. "How do you like your eggs?"

"Scrambled, please."

"I still can't get over your liking cats better than dogs," she began companionably. "All my life I've been hearing about a boy and his dog, never about a boy and his cat."

"How about Dick Whittington?" demanded Brad with a teasing glance up at his aunt as she slipped the bread into the toaster.

"That's right," she acknowledged in a surprised voice.

"And then, of course, there's Puss in Boots and the fake Marquis of Carabas. And *Benjamin West and His Cat, Grimalkin*. And *The Cat Who Went to Heaven* and the poor artist."

From the stove, Mrs. Cary looked around at her nephew with a new respect. "You've read something besides space books, I can see that."

"Well, sure," said Brad, and for the first time his voice had a boy's hearty ring to it. He measured her with a thoughtful eye as she set the breakfast on the table. "I even like the Freddy books now and then," he confessed. "But of course they're kid stuff now."

"I've never read them," Mrs. Cary admitted frankly. "But I still love the *Just So Stories*. I consider 'The Cat That Walked by Himself' one of the most astute documents on domesticity I ever read."

"It's okay," said Brad. " 'Rikki-Tikki-Tavi' is better, though."

Mrs. Cary leaned back in her chair and surveyed her nephew with a frankly admiring expression. "I can see that we have a strong bond between us," she said happily. "If I'd known you loved books, I'd never have feared your coming at all."

Brad looked up in amazement. "You mean you were afraid to have me?"

She nodded, looking shamefaced. "That was part of it. You see, I don't know anything about children and I guess I'm sort of afraid of them. I didn't know what I would *do* with you. I thought you might be dreadfully bored and would resent me."

Brad nodded understandingly. "Do you know any kids? Besides this Cricket, I mean."

Mrs. Cary shook her head. "I've only been here a few weeks, and outside of the neighbors I don't know anyone. I've been busy getting settled, of course."

"Any kids living around here?" asked Brad.

"Not that I've noticed. Crow's Harbor is sort of an old person's village. We're all retired, more or less. However," she added brightly, "The Cat has mentioned children on the beach during the summer, so I suppose you'll meet some there."

A silence fell between them, and then Brad said, "What else has The Cat told you?"

Mrs. Cary looked out of the window, considering. At last she said, "A stranger dropped in one evening about a week ago and wanted to use the phone. He had come to see Mrs. Crow, who used to live here but died a few months ago. The

Cat was here at the time (in fact it all happened the very night The Cat moved in) and he told me next morning that he thought the man might be a smuggler." She spoke seriously and, as she finished, looked intently into Brad's eyes for the effect of her words upon him. It was hardly what she had expected.

Brad had just taken a swallow of milk and as she finished speaking he chortled and choked. Quickly he pressed his napkin to his face, and his eyes, dancing merrily, met hers above it. When he could speak he said, "Honest, Aunt Cary you're just as crazy as Dad and Mom said you were."

He sounded utterly pleased, but Mrs. Cary's tone was ominous as she asked, "What did they mean, 'crazy'?"

Brad shook his head quickly. "They didn't mean anything bad; they just said you had a crazy sense of humor, and you sure have."

He chewed a piece of toast meditatively. When he had swallowed it he said, like one bestowing his highest compliment, "You may *be* old, but you sure don't *talk* old."

"Well, thank you for nothing," said Mrs. Cary. "For your information, I'm just ten years older than your father."

"Gosh!" returned Brad, surveying his aunt with eyes suddenly sober, and Mrs. Cary was sure she had said the wrong thing.

"How about a piece of cake?" she asked, glad to change the subject.

"For breakfast?"

"Why not? I've heard a great deal about eating pie for breakfast in Maine. Why not cake in Crow's Harbor?"

"It's okay with me," declared Brad heartily.

While Mrs. Cary did the dishes, her guest got dressed. By the time she joined him in his bedroom, he had spread up his bed and the big metal suitcase was open on the floor. Two piles of books were stacked on the floor beside it, and Brad motioned toward them as she entered the room.

"Where'll we put these?"

There were no bookshelves in the bedroom.

"I'll make room for them on the shelves in the living room," she said.

"If you have some bricks and a couple of boards, I can make shelves right in here," Brad offered. "Dad's study is fixed that way."

"Why, Brad, that's a wonderful idea. I remember those shelves your father made. I don't know what may be out in that old shed Mrs. Crow used for a garage. But if you don't find what you need, we'll jolly well get it."

"Then I'll just leave the books here."

Together they sorted and put away the clothes, and by the time they had finished with the contents of the suitcase it looked as if Brad had really settled in to stay. There were even writing paper, a ball-point pen, and a book of stamps on the little table under the garden window. Brad looked around happily.

"It's going to be fun having my own room."

"You share yours with Dick, as I remember," said Mrs. Cary. Dick was Brad's older brother.

All at once she laughed with sudden relief. "Already you've found one good thing about Three Corners. You can have your own room here."

"I've found two good things," Brad corrected her.

"What's the other?" she asked quickly, hopefully.

"The Cat."

"Oh, yes. Of course, The Cat."

Promptly at eleven o'clock the flap over the cat hole flashed open violently to reveal a patch of bright light as The Cat came streaking into the house pursued by a roar which was choked off suddenly.

"Cricket has arrived," called Mrs. Cary as she hurried to open the front door.

This time Cricket had been prepared for The Cat and was holding Doc on a tight leash.

"Grandy says Brad is here." She greeted Mrs. Cary.

"That he is. Won't you come in?"

Cricket hesitated. "Both of us?"

Mrs. Cary smiled. "Unless you've brought along a steel chain to tie him up with."

Cricket shook her head and returned the smile.

"Then come in," said Mrs. Cary, "both of you."

Brad had been sprawled on the sofa when The Cat made his entry, and was trying to coax him into his lap. But with the arrival of Doc in the entry hall The Cat was off the sofa in a flash and clawing his way to the top of the bookshelves. Up he climbed, knocking off books as he went, until at last he was safely settled between a small reproduction of the "Winged Victory" and a pewter mug.

Brad leaped to his feet. "Get that cat-killer out of here," he yelled, facing Cricket furiously.

"He is not a cat-killer," she yelled right back at him. "He's never killed a cat in his whole life. He only wants to."

"It's the same thing," declared Brad, "because someday

he will. But it had better not be The Cat—and he'd better not *try* to kill him, either."

"Children, children," Mrs. Cary broke in, "that's enough. Brad, I'm shocked that you should dare to speak in such a way to a guest in my house. I demand an apology."

For a moment, boy and woman faced each other without flinching, then Brad dropped his eyes, mumbling, "I'm sorry."

"Good," said Mrs. Cary quickly. "Now," she began brightly, "let's start all over again. Cricket, this is my nephew, Brad Willets, from Lawrence, Kansas. Brad, this is Cricket Mobray, whose grandfather very kindly brought you home last evening."

The two children glanced belligerently at each other, dutifully said, "Hi," and sat down.

For the next moment or two all eyes were on The Cat, who appeared to be the most poised member of the group, and while the others scrambled around in their minds for something appropriate to say, he broke the awkward silence. "I predict a wonderful summer for us all," he announced quietly.

Immediately Doc went into another frenzy. When Cricket had at last subdued him, Mrs. Cary directed a stern eye up to The Cat.

"I care nothing at all for your predictions," she informed him, "and I want you to stop exciting that dog. Not another word out of you. Do you hear?"

"I hear," replied The Cat almost nonchalantly. "And before you get too carried away with yourself, you might do something about that dog. If you don't, I'll be forced to."

Again Doc lunged toward the bookshelves, and this time Brad had to help hold him because Cricket was almost helpless with laughter. The Cat had mewed so exactly on cue that it did seem almost as if he were defying Mrs. Cary.

When things were quiet again, Cricket asked, "What did you think The Cat was predicting, Mrs. Cary? You said you didn't care about his predictions. What were they?"

"He was being sarcastic," explained Mrs. Cary. "What he actually said was 'I predict a wonderful summer for us all.' And there's no *think* about it; that's exactly what he said."

Cricket giggled and looked across at Brad, who was smiling grudgingly.

"And I might add," continued Mrs. Cary, surveying Cricket gravely, "he also said that unless I did something about your dog he was going to."

"I wonder what he could do," Cricket said musingly, looking down with pride at Doc's powerfully muscled body.

"I have no idea," returned Mrs. Cary, "but I am sure The Cat is resourceful. As I think I've intimated to Brad, he is no ordinary cat."

She rose and started toward the kitchen. "I'll leave you two for a little while." Over her shoulder she said, "Cricket and I thought you might enjoy a picnic on the beach this first day, Brad."

Left alone, the children eyed The Cat in order to avoid looking at each other. No word passed between them for at least a minute, and then Cricket spoke, voicing what was uppermost in her mind.

"It's funny you don't like dogs."

"What's funny about it? I happen to hate 'em, that's all."

"But why?"

Brad thought a moment. "Because I've got a paper route,

I guess. You'd hate dogs too if you had a paper route."

"What's that got to do with it?"

Brad sent her a dark look. "They run after your bike and bite your legs, and all you can do is kick out at 'em, and, oh, I don't know, I just hate dogs."

Cricket reached out to stroke Doc's smooth head where it rested on her lap in a direct line with The Cat.

"Doc isn't a bit that way," she declared. "He only chases cats. I've never seen him even look at a boy on a bicycle."

"Well, he'd better not chase The Cat any more," said Brad threateningly.

Their eyes again followed Doc's to where The Cat sat comfortably crouched between the "Winged Victory" and the pewter mug. His eyes were slits, his paws tucked back against his chest. His sides moved evenly in and out as he purred contentedly.

"I think," said Cricket, "that The Cat is able to take care of himself."

Brad didn't reply to this, and a silence hung between them which lasted until Mrs. Cary came in with their lunch bags.

"Here you are," she said, handing a bag to each. "Stay as long as you like, but don't walk too far this first day, Brad. Walking in the sand is hard work; it can make a half a mile seem like two or three."

As soon as they had gone, she went over to the bookshelves.

"You can come down now," she said.

Without a word The Cat rose and, having measured the distance between him and the sofa, took a long, graceful leap and landed. From that vantage point he watched, with Mrs. Cary, the boy and girl plodding across the beach. Doc,

free once more, was racing along the edge of the breakers, a cloud of sandpipers skimming before him.

"He's a nice kid," observed The Cat.

Mrs. Cary looked down quickly at him. "That's the truth, but I never expected to hear you say it."

"Never judge a person till you meet him," said The Cat. "I was wrong about Brad. He's the first person I ever met who liked me on sight simply because I am what I am—a cat."

"Really!" exclaimed Mrs. Cary. "That explains why you accepted him so quickly. Naturally, I was amazed."

"I know what you mean," said The Cat. "I'm really a
little amazed myself. But when he came up the walk last
night it suddenly struck me how alone he was and how alone
I was, and a kind of sympathy seemed to pass between us. It's
very hard to explain, dear lady, but suddenly I positively
wanted him to like me."

"Well, it was mighty decent of you to help him over his
first night away from home. I want you to know that I appreciate it."

The Cat lifted one paw and started to lick it, then set it
down again.

"If you really mean that, there is always a sure way to show your appreciation—at least to a cat."

Mrs. Cary, smiling, swung her eyes away from the window and down to The Cat again.

"The best in the house shall be yours," she told him.

Together they crossed the room toward the kitchen, with The Cat walking just ahead of his mistress, his tail straight and high.

11

THE CAT TAKES OVER

The picnic ended in disaster, and it was nearly two weeks before Cricket was seen again at Three Corners. Then she appeared only because she was summoned. Anyone who knew anything at all about children should have known that the last thing Brad and Cricket desired that morning was more of each other's company. Brad would have enjoyed a picnic alone but certainly did not at all want to share one with this strange girl and her odious dog. Cricket, though she had behaved very decently toward him, still resented Brad's dislike of all dogs, and especially of Doc. But what could the children do? A well-meaning grown-up whom they both respected had planned this unfortunate outing for them, and they had no choice but to go along. This didn't mean, however, that they had to be polite to each other. And as they plodded across the sands under the eyes of The Cat and Mrs. Cary their conversation was grudging. They were both heartily thankful when at last their lunch bags were empty and their responsibility to Mrs. Cary's picnic was at an end.

Even so, they might, with Mrs. Cary's prodding, have ironed out their differences and put behind them the unfortunate circumstances of their first meeting, except for the disaster already referred to.

They had chosen to have their lunch on some rocks at a distance down the beach. By the time they had finished and carefully disposed of the waste in a trash can, Brad had decided that, with the walk back, he would have had enough of the beach for that day. Cricket knew that it was time for her to report back to her grandfather, and, since the shortest way to the village lay up the beach and along the road past Three Corners, the two started back together.

It was when they had cleared the sands and had almost gained the road along the cliff that the disaster occurred.

Except during the period when he had sat attentively in front of them, begging for handouts, Doc had been running free from the moment they had left the house. Now he was galloping easily ahead of them, and not until they had nearly gained the road did Cricket suddenly remember The Cat. But then it was too late.

Even as she screamed, "*Doc*," the big dog gathered his powerful hindquarters for the mighty spring that would catapult him across the road.

The Cat, as was his custom, had been sitting watchfully at the end of the walk and so was the first thing Doc saw as his head came above the cliff. Without a sound he leaped, and without a sound The Cat started his run for the cat hole.

This time, however, Doc was not to be thwarted by that old maneuver. Cutting through the front garden, he came between The Cat and the house. The Cat, aware of the dog's intention, spun instantly and headed for the back garden, where the tallest trees grew. This brought Doc around in a circle so tight it threw him onto one flank. Then he was up and after The Cat. But the momentary halt had given that animal the lead he needed, and Doc vented his fury at the failure of his plan in a frenzy of mingled howls and barks.

Brad and Cricket, rushing at top speed, rounded the corner of the house and crashed up to the gate leading to the back garden. They were just in time to see The Cat speed without halt up the trunk of the first tree, in a lovely fluid motion that propelled him forward and up at exactly the speed he had been maintaining on the ground. Then it happened.

Doc was going too fast to stop, although he tried, as his skid marks later proved. There was a sickening thud, and Doc dropped flat. In the ensuing silence The Cat looked curiously down from the safety of the first stout limb and studied his recent adversary now stretched motionless beneath him.

The silence was broken by a pitiful wail. "Doc, oh, Doc, you're killed." And Cricket fumbled blindly at the gate latch, her eyes too dimmed with tears to see what she was doing.

Brad pushed her aside and opened the gate. "Serves him right if he is," he said cruelly, just as Mrs. Cary came running from the house.

"What on earth has happened?" she demanded, kneeling with Cricket at Doc's side.

"I forgot to put the leash on him and he saw The Cat and took after him, and now he's dead." Cricket sobbed. Slowly she stroked the still black body spotted here and there with her tears.

Trying to determine what had happened, Mrs. Cary lifted her eyes to where The Cat lay along the limb, as relaxed as if he had been there all morning.

"I said I'd do something about that dog if he didn't let me alone," he answered her inquiring gaze.

Instantly one of Doc's hind legs began to twitch. Next, his eyes opened.

"He's coming to," announced Brad without enthusiasm.

"Oh, Doc." Cricket whimpered, taking his great head in her arms. "Don't die; please don't die."

Mrs. Cary, who had never wrung her hands in her whole life, felt very much like wringing them now. She hovered over Cricket and the damaged dog, feeling perfectly helpless and even a little sympathetic toward The Cat. One couldn't actually blame a creature for trying to save his own life, and Doc *had* started all the fuss. Still, she would hate very much to see as nice a child as Cricket lose something she prized as much as Doc.

Presently Doc began to make feeble efforts to free himself from Cricket's embrace, and when she let him go he rose shakily to his feet. He would live.

"Now maybe he'll learn to let The Cat alone," observed Brad, "and about time, too, if you ask me."

Cricket was on her feet like a flash and facing him. "I think you're hateful. Perfectly hateful. And I wish I'd never heard of you."

She snapped the leash onto Doc's collar and began leading him away, but Mrs. Cary stepped to her side quickly and put an arm around her shoulders. "You don't really mean that, Cricket."

"I do too," returned Cricket fiercely, but she didn't shake off Mrs. Cary's arm.

"When all is said and done," continued Mrs. Cary in a matter-of-fact tone, "it happened because you forgot to put the leash on Doc. Isn't that right?"

Cricket didn't reply, and Mrs. Cary gave her a very slight shake. "Isn't it?" she persisted.

"I guess so," Cricket mumbled.

"Well, then," said Mrs. Cary, sounding vastly relieved, "there's really nothing for you to lose your temper over. Since you think so much of Doc, you can understand how Brad and I might feel if he got his teeth into The Cat. It is, after all, my cat, you know. I think, therefore, you should forgive Brad for what he said in the heat of the moment." She swung Cricket around to face Brad, who still stood where Doc had fallen. "Just as I think he should forgive you for letting Doc scare The Cat."

Across the intervening space, Brad and Cricket mumbled a reluctant "Okay" to each other. Indistinct and halfhearted as it was, it seemed to satisfy Mrs. Cary.

"Now," she said, just as if nothing had happened, "if we could only get Doc and The Cat to make up, we wouldn't ever have anything more to worry about in that direction, would we?"

A voice answered quietly from the heights above them. "You have nothing to worry about on that score anyway, dear lady. If I know dogs, and I think I do, that one won't be bothering me for a good long while, if ever."

Mrs. Cary glanced up at The Cat, noting how his tail, having slid off the limb, waved back and forth in the breeze.

"I certainly hope you're right," she answered.

"Hope who's right?" demanded Brad at once, a hopeful look on his face.

"Why, The Cat," replied his aunt. "Didn't you just hear him? He said that Doc is not likely to bother him any more."

As usual, Brad found this very funny, but no answering gleam of amusement appeared this time on Cricket's face. To her such levity so soon after Doc's nearly fatal accident was the ultimate in unfeelingness. She wanted no part of either of these people and shook off Mrs. Cary's arm almost rudely.

"Why, Cricket, what on earth—" began Mrs. Cary.

"I think you're both perfectly horrid," cried Cricket chokingly. "It's no joke when a person's dog almost gets killed."

"But I wasn't joking." Mrs. Cary tried to explain. "The Cat did actually say that."

Cricket looked at her witheringly and began to walk toward the garden gate, Doc following meekly behind her. Mrs. Cary had no choice but to let her go. How could she ever make Cricket understand that The Cat was no ordinary cat? If only she knew a little more about children!

Cricket opened the gate and started to go through it when again The Cat spoke.

"That dog isn't up to walking back to town, not till he's over his headache anyway. He must have a bump as big as a pigeon's egg on the top of his noggin. What he needs is a drink of water, an aspirin, and a good long rest."

"Cricket," called Mrs. Cary, walking quickly toward her, "Cricket, come back, dear. I'm sorry if I hurt your feelings; and I'm sorry Doc got hurt. Really, I am."

Cricket paused and looked around at her.

"Actually that dog has had a hard wallop, and I don't think you should be walking him to town right away." She leaned over and felt the Doberman's head. He winced away from her fingers. "He's got a lump as big as a pigeon's egg. Here, feel it." Cricket gently laid her fingers on the poor head and looked across Doc at Mrs. Cary, her face full of concern. "I think you should give Doc a drink of water and an aspirin. And then he should have a chance to rest."

Cricket looked less militant.

"Why don't we all come inside and have a Coke and settle down with a book while Doc sleeps off his headache?"

Cricket shook her head. "My grandfather will be wondering where I am," she said. "Thanks just the same, but I'll walk very slowly and I think Doc will be all right."

"Here's Joe again," announced The Cat from his tree.

Mrs. Cary glanced toward the road. A car was coming slowly around the corner, and the driver was peering into the garden.

"That's the second time he's been by today," The Cat said, but Mrs. Cary, having learned her lesson, paid no attention to him.

All at once Brad let out a cry. "Hey," he yelled at the man in the car. "Hey, wait."

To his aunt he explained, "That's the man who was driving the car last night when Cricket's grandfather brought me home. They were together."

The man stopped the car and Brad ran through the gate and up to him, calling, "Could you take a girl and a dog back to town? The dog got his head bumped pretty hard, and the girl has to get back to her grandfather." The man said something, and Brad turned to yell at Cricket, "What did you say your last name was?"

"Mobray," said Cricket.

Brad came running back. "He'll take you," he told Cricket.

"That's very kind of him," said Mrs. Cary. "Come on, Cricket." To Brad she said, "You stay here; the walk back would be too much for you after the beach. I shan't be long."

"But Aunt Cary," protested Brad, "I tell you he knows Cricket's grandfather; he was with him last night."

"I don't doubt it at all," declared Mrs. Cary, "but as far as I am concerned this gentleman is a perfect stranger, and Cricket will *not* ride back to town with him alone. At least," she muttered to herself as she followed Cricket out to the car, "I know that much about children."

Besides, suppose The Cat were right and this was Joe? And suppose he were a smuggler? Why had he been past Three Corners twice in one day? Now was her chance to study this Joe.

Cricket and Doc got into the back seat, and Mrs. Cary got in beside the driver. They had hardly started up when Cricket said, "I've seen you at the pet shop where I buy Doc's food."

"That's right," said the man.

"How come you know my grandfather?" asked Cricket.

"Just know him, that's all," returned the man.

"Have you lived at Crow's Harbor very long?" asked Mrs. Cary, taking a good look at the man's profile.

"Off and on," returned the man, and she wondered if he was deliberately evading their questions.

"I am Mrs. Cary."

"Yeah, I know," said the man, not taking his eyes off the road or mentioning his own name.

Mrs. Cary settled back. "It's very good of you to give Cricket and her dog a lift into town. The dog chased my cat up a tree and ran head on into it. Got quite a bump, poor thing." She looked around and smiled sympathetically at Cricket, who smiled a small smile back. Doc lay with his head in her lap.

The man said nothing. In silence the three rode to the edge of the village, and then the man said over his shoulder to Cricket, "Where you want to get off at?"

"At Santee's Shanties, if it's not too much trouble."

The man swung the car around a corner and in another minute had pulled to the curb alongside the motel.

They got out and thanked him, and the car pulled away.

A man was coming out of one of the cottages, and Cricket called to him, "Grandy, do we have any aspirin?"

Mrs. Cary turned, then gasped in astonishment. The man approaching them, the man whom Cricket had hailed as "Grandy," was none other than her mysterious caller of the night The Cat moved in, the man named Mo.

"Grandy, this is Mrs. Cary," said Cricket.

"I've met Mrs. Cary," said her grandfather, smiling as he extended his hand.

Mrs. Cary took it and tried to return his warm handclasp. "How do you do?" she murmured.

"Still got that cat?" he demanded, chuckling.

Mrs. Cary nodded.

"Is it still talking about smugglers?"

Mrs. Cary felt her face growing warm, but she faced Mr. Mobray bravely. "As a matter of fact, he is," she said levelly.

The man laughed as if at a good joke. He reached out to pull Cricket up to his side. "How did you and Brad make out?"

"We didn't," said Cricket promptly. "I hate him and he hates dogs and that's that."

She explained to her grandfather somewhat breathlessly all that had happened, with Mrs. Cary filling in the gaps. When the recital was over and Grandy had examined Doc's bump and ordered an aspirin, she said good-by to Mrs. Cary and led him to the cottage.

"May I drive you home?" asked Mr. Mobray after she had gone.

Mrs. Cary shook her head. "Thank you just the same, but I feel as if, after all the excitement of the last hour, a quiet walk home is just what I need."

They parted with friendly nods and smiles, but as Mrs. Cary walked slowly home she had much to think about. Why had Mo, Mr. Mobray, appeared at Three Corners that night in the company of Joe? Why had they been together again in her area of the village on Brad's first night here? And why was Joe circling Three Corners again today? And what was the reason for Mr. Mobray's interest in the departed Mrs. Crow? It was she he had been seeking that evening. Cricket had said he was here investigating something.

She was so involved in meditation that she almost failed to return the major's greeting as she came abreast of the Willoughby garden.

"A penny for your thoughts, dear lady," he shouted jocularly as she belatedly returned his "How-de-do."

"They're worth more than that, major," she called back pleasantly, hurrying by.

It seemed highly doubtful to her that the searchlight of the major's curiosity could do much to penetrate the gathering cloud of mystery now threatening to envelop Three Corners and everyone connected with it.

Besides, she had walked so slowly that Brad might have begun to worry about her.

12

PROBLEMS

During the days immediately following Doc's disaster, Mrs. Cary tried to telephone Cricket to discover how the poor dog was. But since there were no telephones in the cottages, and since her messages left at the office were either never delivered or else ignored, she decided to call at Santee's Shanties in person. There was always the possibility that the Mobrays had suddenly left town. So on her next trip to the village Mrs. Cary walked over to the motel. She learned that Cricket and her grandfather were still living there, but both of them were out. After leaving still another message, Mrs. Cary went regretfully away.

When a week had gone without a sign of the girl or her dog, Mrs. Cary said to Brad as they sat waiting for the mail one morning, "I'm afraid Cricket has crossed us off her list of favorite people."

"That's okay with me," grumbled her nephew, not lifting his eyes from his book.

"Well, it's not okay with me," returned Mrs. Cary from her chair beside the window, where she was sewing buttons on one of Brad's shirts. Every shirt requiring buttons had one or two missing or hanging by a thread, so she had gone straight through his clothes closet, snatching as she went, and making those little insect noises that were a habit with her. "Sst. Sst." Fortunately most of Brad's upper garments, including pajama tops, slipped over the head. "It's not okay with me at all," she repeated now, biting off a thread. "I like Cricket very much and I regret that she apparently dislikes me."

Brad looked up from his book. "But how can you like her so much? You said yourself you'd only seen her once before the day Doc got hurt."

"I know," agreed Mrs. Cary, "but that was enough to let me know that Cricket is an honest, forthright, courageous, and dependable child. I like her very much."

Brad stared at his aunt for one full minute before he said, "Gosh, Aunt Cary, you sure find out an awful lot about people awful quick."

"Perhaps I do," she replied.

He closed his book, keeping a finger between the pages. His eyes were teasing as he surveyed his aunt.

"What was that again you said about Cricket?"

Mrs. Cary threw him a suspicious glance, but answered, "I said she was honest, forthright, courageous, and dependable."

"She's also bad-tempered, opinionated, a dog-lover, and a girl," he countered.

"She's certainly a dog-lover and a girl, but that can't reasonably be held against her," argued Mrs. Cary. "As to her being bad-tempered, I am by no means convinced that she is, nor that she is opinionated. She certainly has her own ideas about dogs and cats, but that's her privilege."

Brad considered this for a moment, then said, "All right. Prove that she's honest, and all the rest. How do you know?"

"I know she's honest by the very way she looks at you," answered Mrs. Cary. "Her eyes are always direct, as if she had nothing to hide. And she speaks her mind without being smart-alecky about it."

"I'll say she speaks her mind," said Brad grimly. "Mom would have smacked me for talking to you the way she did."

"Not in the circumstances, I think," said Mrs. Cary. "Cricket was terribly upset. She was frightened for Doc and in no condition to judge a situation, or the people in it."

"All right, so she's honest," conceded Brad. "What do you mean, 'forthright'?"

Mrs. Cary put down her sewing and let her gaze rest on the view of the sea outside her window. It was another sunny morning, with the water intensely blue.

"It's a little hard to define what I mean by 'forthright,' Brad. It's a straightforward quality some people have, and it's somehow mixed up with honesty too. People who are forthright seem to know their ground and to stand firmly on it. I suppose sometimes it can seem tactless, but I'm sure it's always honest." She turned to him suddenly. "What does the dictionary say?"

Brad rose from the sofa and crossed the room to where the worn old Webster sat on the wide window sill. It was the same sill The Cat had crossed to make his first entry into Mrs. Cary's home. Brad opened the heavy book and began flipping its pages.

"Here we are," he announced at last and proceeded to read.

"It doesn't say quite the same thing about 'forthright' that you do, does it?" Brad observed.

"Not quite," admitted Mrs. Cary. "Yet when I talk about a forthright person I know exactly what I mean. It's a feeling I get that is a whole lot bigger than a mere definition." She turned to him eagerly. "That's the exciting thing about words, Brad. They convey so much more of your feelings than they actually state. I just love words."

"They're okay," allowed Brad. A silence fell between them before he asked in rather a small voice, "Would you say I was a forthright person?"

She looked squarely over at him, and his eyes met hers. He had returned to the sofa, and flung himself onto it with one leg up and one leg down.

"Oh, yes, Brad, and more. I'd say you were a courageous person too."

Brad gave an irreverent hoot. "*Courageous?* That's the craziest thing you've said yet, Aunt Cary. When have you ever seen me being courageous?"

Before answering, she turned the shirt over on her lap, saw where a seam on the collar had opened, and began stitching it.

"You came here against your wishes," she began, "and you have made the best of it. In fact, during the last couple of days I've begun to get the impression that you were even beginning to enjoy yourself. It takes a very special kind of courage to make the best of things, my dear."

Another silence hung between them, and then Brad said, "Getting back to Cricket, why do you think she's courageous?"

"The way she handles that brute of a dog, for one thing.

For another, I happen to know that she would like nothing better than a chance to see the ghost which she believes inhabits this house."

Brad straightened up, his eyes bright with interest.

"A ghost! Here?"

Mrs. Cary nodded. "It was the ghost that brought Cricket here in the first place." While she completed the work on the collar, she informed her nephew of what Cricket had told her.

"Have you ever seen the ghost?" Brad asked when she had finished.

"No," said Mrs. Cary.

"Ever smelled the sandalwood?"

Mrs. Cary shook her head. She looked doubtfully across at Brad. "Perhaps I shouldn't have mentioned the ghost."

"I don't really believe in 'em," Brad reassured her. "It's fun, though, thinking about a haunted house—you know, buried treasure, creaks and groans in the dark of the night, and maybe the rattle of a chain."

Mrs. Cary shuddered. "I don't believe in them either, of course. Just the same if I ever get a whiff of sandalwood around this place I'm going to take off from here so fast that there won't be any trace of me but the dust of my passing."

Brad chuckled; then he grew thoughtful. "Where can a person buy sandalwood?" he asked innocently, but his aunt was too sharp for him.

"Brad." She shook a finger at him as she rose from her chair, the shirt finished and folded in her hand. *"Don't you dare, young man. Don't you dare!"*

Brad fell into a heap on the sofa, convulsed at the thought of his venerable aunt scared out of her bed and house in the middle of the night by a whiff of store-bought sandalwood.

The sound of Mr. Norton's station wagon at the row of mailboxes brought him up from his gleeful chortlings. He was off the sofa and out the front door before the car's dust had had a chance to settle.

Mrs. Cary looked after him, smiling. They never had got around to Cricket's dependability!

Since Mrs. Cary almost never got a letter, and since some member of his family wrote to him every day, Brad had taken on the pleasant chore of picking up the mail. So it was to him this morning that Major Paddleford spoke as he came up in the wake of the station wagon's departure.

"Good morning, young man."

"Good morning, Major," returned Brad.

"Lovely morning," declared the Major, studying the boy closely. He passed a finger over his mustache before announcing, "You're putting on weight, my lad."

Mrs. Melton and Mrs. Kane had just come up, and Brad wished the major would keep his opinions to himself. But the major did quite the contrary. He turned to the ladies as if seeking their corroboration of his statement.

"Ever see such a change in a youngster?" he demanded of them, at which they agreed immediately that they never had, and Brad felt his face reddening.

"You have more color too," the major boomed.

Brad turned quickly to his aunt's mailbox and yanked it open. Sure enough, his letter was lying there, along with *The Big City Daily*.

He tore the letter open, standing with his back to the major and the others, hoping they would leave before any more

observations could be passed on his appearance. He heard the ladies move off, but the major remained, and at last only the two of them were left standing beside the row of boxes.

"It just occurred to me" began the major, talking for once in an almost surreptitious manner, "you've had a week of female companionship, and I was wondering if it might not be time for a change. Now that the Willoughbys are away, I get rather lonesome. In short, my boy, I'd be very glad of your company any time—any time at all."

Brad hardly knew how to answer. Fleeting memories of tucking in the neighborhood went through his mind and he didn't think he'd care for any more of that. He had never found his grandfather's company immensely entertaining, and they had a whole lifetime's acquaintance between them. What could he find to do or talk about with this old stranger? Still, the major undoubtedly meant to be kind. Brad was framing a polite reply when he spoke again.

"I have a TV set, you know."

"You have?" returned Brad, his face registering sudden interest.

"We get only one channel in Crow's Harbor," the major went on, "but I believe it offers a fair sampling of the leading programs—baseball, of course, at this season." His eyes under their frosty brows bored into Brad's, finding what they sought there, for Brad's face had lit.

"I'll have to ask my aunt."

"She doesn't have one, then, I take it," said the major, foraging successfully.

"No," said Brad.

"Then by all means ask her, dear boy. No reason in the world why you should be missing your TV programs. No reason at all."

Brad hastened across the road with the unread letter in his hands. It was from Agatha anyway, and, though she meant well, she was only eight.

"Aunt Cary," he yelled as soon as he was inside, "can I go over to the major's to watch TV?"

Mrs. Cary came out of the kitchen. "What's this about the major and TV?"

Brad explained.

"I wish that old busybody would mind his own business," she snapped, and Brad's face began to grow sullen.

"Then I can't go?"

"No, you can't."

Brad swung around, his feet barely missing the hall stand holding the telephone. "Gee whiz, Aunt Cary, I can't just sit here with you all day. The major's a nice old guy. And there's *baseball*."

He flung himself onto the sofa with a miserable, "Gosh."

"What about all those books you dragged out here?" she asked. "What about being an astronaut? How are you ever going to become something like that if you sit all day in front of TV? Furthermore, you were sent here to get ocean breezes and outdoor exercise."

He rose to his knees on the sofa and looked over the top of it at her, a hopeful gleam in his eye.

"Good gosh, Aunt Cary. You don't suppose I want to look at it all the time? Just now and then—like, for instance, a baseball game, and a real good Western. Only an idiot could look at it all the time."

"How do you handle it at home?" asked Mrs. Cary.

Brad hitched toward her on the sofa, his shoelaces creaking as he dragged them across its brocaded cushions. "On school nights we can only look at it for thirty minutes. That's all— just thirty minutes. During vacation only two hours out of the twenty-four, unless it's baseball, or a rocket's going up, or the President's talking, or something special like that."

"I suppose you've been missing it hideously, then," said Mrs. Cary, looking thoughtfully at him.

Brad shrugged. "Yeah, sort of. But I just figured it was only two hours anyway, and I've spent that time on the beach."

"I see," said Mrs. Cary. They looked at each other for a long moment. At last she said, "As long as the major has been kind enough to offer you his hospitality, and as long as your family has no objections to your watching TV, I hardly see how I can refuse to let you accept his offer."

"You mean I can, then?" cried Brad, springing off the sofa.

"Yes, you may. But only for one hour out of twenty-four and never in the evening."

"But the best programs are in the evening," wailed Brad.

"I'm sorry," said Mrs. Cary. "But you are not going to spend any evening out of this house unless I am with you, and I can assure you that I have no intention of watching TV with Major Paddleford—or with anyone else, for that matter."

"But the baseball games take more than an hour, Aunt Cary. You wouldn't expect me to come home in the middle of a game."

"I suppose not," said Mrs. Cary, looking greatly bewildered.

"Then if it's a baseball game I can stay until it's over?" he begged.

Slowly she nodded. "I guess so," she conceded reluctantly. Then her voice grew firm. "But not at night. If it's a night game, you can't see it, that's all."

Brad knew when it was useless to say more. And so it was settled.

13

WILD CAT
COVE

On the following day the Bookmobile arrived at Three Corners. Mrs. Cary, watching the time, saw its brown bulk sweep to a stop beside the back garden and felt the little glow of pleasure its arrival always gave her. Here were fresh books again. What excitement would its shelves offer her this week? What far places would beckon her interest? What new lives would she be invited to explore? And what fun it was to visit this roving library! Though its book collection was necessarily limited, still, Mrs. Cary couldn't help liking above all others a library which parked itself once a week alongside her own garden.

Three Corners happened to be the logical place for the Bookmobile to set up business, since it marked the junction of three roads. By a happy coincidence this stop, with its fine view of the sea, came near noon, and it was here Miss Temple, the librarian-driver, ate her lunch.

Brad was at the major's when the Bookmobile arrived.

I wonder if I should phone him, Mrs. Cary said to herself.

Though he had by no means exhausted his books on space science, she had gathered the notion lately that he might welcome some other reading. She had suggested as much, and Brad had agreed that more variety might be a good thing.

"Astronauts have to be very well-rounded people," he had informed her, and asked in the next breath, "Do they have baseball stories on the Bookmobile?"

So now she started toward the entry hall. But halfway there she stopped and shook her head. No, she wouldn't phone Brad after all. Before he left the house this morning she had told him when the Bookmobile was due to arrive. If he chose to ignore it for TV, that was his business. Besides, she wouldn't want the major to think she was nagging her nephew. The limits of his TV viewing were thoroughly understood among the three of them. Within those limits, she felt she had no right to interfere. Meanwhile, she could pick up a baseball story or two with the hope that Brad hadn't already read them.

She gathered up the books she had borrowed last week and started with them across the back garden and through the gate. People were converging upon the Bookmobile from several roads away. Some were in cars and many were afoot, but all came eagerly, with books in their arms, and Miss Temple greeted each one like an old friend.

"I see we have a new borrower today," she observed, looking past Mrs. Cary as she came up the steps. Her eyes were so merry that Mrs. Cary turned to see what could be amusing Miss Temple so much.

There at the end of the line, exactly as if he were awaiting his turn to climb aboard, stood—The Cat.

"Oh, dear!" exclaimed Mrs. Cary.

"I think *The Tailor of Gloucester* would be about the right size for him," said Miss Temple. "And he'd probably be able to identify completely with Simpkin."

Good-natured laughter greeted Miss Temple's fooling, and other titles were suggested for The Cat's reading all up and down the line.

"You'd better go home, sir," Mrs. Cary called down to him. To Miss Temple she said, "I didn't know he was following me here. I'll keep an eye on him."

"Don't worry about him," returned the librarian easily, taking books and stacking them in the bin beside her. "He won't be the first cat that's tried to take a ride with us. Usually they shoot out as soon as I start the motor."

Mrs. Cary moved along the shelves, reading the rows of titles, but they conveyed little to her mind. Her eyes kept darting uneasily toward the door. While she didn't actually believe The Cat would come inside, still she felt jumpy about him. If he did come in, would he follow her out? Probably not, as The Cat rarely did what you wanted him to. Would she be able to pick him up, then, and carry him out? She never had picked him up, and though she had seen Brad do it once or twice, she doubted seriously that The Cat would tolerate such familiarity from her. Even in Brad's arms he had seemed decidedly unsettled. Yet she would prefer to make the attempt at capturing him to having him sneak in and, unobserved, be carried off to some distant part of the county.

The truth was that, though she often found him annoying, as she did now, Mrs. Cary had no wish to lose The Cat. Lately he had begun to fill a once happily vacant niche in her life.

Since Brad's arrival at Three Corners, The Cat's whole

nature had undergone a change. It was nothing short of wonderful, the influence Brad's affection had on that animal. He slept nearly every night on the boy's bed, hung around the house a good deal of the day, and followed Brad everywhere, even to the beach. However, he had not followed him to the major's this morning. Evidently no amount of mellowing would ever alter The Cat's feelings toward the major.

Today, with Brad gone, he had followed his mistress to the Bookmobile, where he seemed quite at home among the group of strangers gathered there. Seeing him, one might almost permit himself the hope that in a few more weeks the tough old fishing Tom might become as relaxed and docile as the gentlest tabby.

From that first night when she had found The Cat curled on Brad's bed, Mrs. Cary had been trying conscientiously to see the animal through the boy's eyes. It was really her first step in an effort to understand this nephew whose guardianship she had assumed for the summer. Whether or not it had resulted in a better understanding of Brad, she wasn't sure. But one thing was certain: she was beginning to have a better understanding of The Cat. She was beginning to see grace in his every movement, to find amusement in his outrageous flattery as mealtime approached; to respect his vigilantly guarded independence at all other times. If pushed, she would have had to admit to a kind of dawning fondness for The Cat.

So now she didn't want him to come aboard the Bookmobile.

Having at last chosen her books, Mrs. Cary had them charged out to her and descended the stairs to the road. She had to place each foot carefully, for her arms were full. Among the volumes were two baseball stories, a collection called *Crack of the Bat* and another book, a whole long story, called *The Kid from Tomkinsville*.

When she reached the ground, she looked around for The Cat. He was sitting toward the rear of the Bookmobile, with his tail wrapped around his front feet, wearing the complacent expression of a cat minding his own business.

"Come on," she said as she passed by him and started to enter the garden.

The Cat never budged, so she paused with her hand on the gate and called to him again.

He turned his head slowly and looked over his shoulder at her for a long moment before turning his head back again.

"I don't want you to go aboard that Bookmobile," she said sharply.

The Cat shuddered the fur along his back but showed no other sign of having heard her.

"All right," said Mrs. Cary. "It's entirely up to you. But it's only fair to warn you that you could get carried to the ends of the county."

The Cat looked around at her again and this time he spoke. "And I'd find my way home again."

Mrs. Cary shrugged and went on into the garden.

"What's with The Cat?" called a familiar voice from the road, and Brad came strolling up.

Mrs. Cary turned to him with a sigh of relief. "Thank heaven you're here, Brad. The Cat followed me to the Bookmobile and now seems to be waiting for a chance to go aboard it. I've told him I didn't want him to, that he could get carried to the ends of the county, but he merely brags that he can find his way home again."

Brad chuckled and squatted down in front The Cat. "He's right, Aunt Cary. Cats have been known to find their way home over thousands of miles."

The Cat offered his chin, and Brad began rubbing it carefully.

"In that case I shall stop worrying about him," said Mrs. Cary. "Look at these two books and tell me what you think of them."

Brad straightened up to read the titles. "Yeah, they're super, both of 'em. You'll like 'em, Aunt Cary."

"I got them for you, Brad."

"For me? Heck, I read 'em ages ago."

"Well then, suppose you come into the Bookmobile with me and pick out a couple for yourself."

"Okay," said Brad, waiting until Mrs. Cary had dumped onto a garden bench the books she wanted to keep.

It was while Brad was inside the Bookmobile making a careful selection of his books that The Cat quietly mounted the short flight of steps and entered the vehicle. He slipped past Brad and Mrs. Cary, who had had to go along with her nephew in order that he might use her library card, evaded the feet of two other borrowers, and crept with unerring accuracy to the only opening in the rows of shelves large enough to accommodate his size. Quickly he turned in this little space at the very end of the shelves and faced front. Anyone observing him—but nobody did—would have known at once that this was not The Cat's first time aboard the Bookmobile.

Finding that he had read the only baseball stories remaining, and feeling that this might be the time to read a book or two about the sea, Brad presented to Miss Temple two books, one *Kon-Tiki*, and the other *The Ship without a Crew*.

"What happened to The Cat?" asked Mrs. Cary as soon as they were outside. "He was sitting here when we went in."

"Probably gone back to the house," said Brad.

"Suppose he went into the Bookmobile!"

Brad shook his head. "I looked all around real carefully before we went out. There was no cat anywhere."

"Good!" said Mrs. Cary, adding irrelevantly, "It's nearly noon; you must be starved."

After lunch Mrs. Cary went upstairs for her nap and Brad settled down on the sofa with one of his library books. After only a few minutes he got up and walked over to the window, where he stood for some time looking out upon the water. After a while he put on his windbreaker and carefully let himself outside.

He crossed the road and descended the cliff to the beach. Having paused only long enough to estimate the distance between him and the long point of land reaching into the water, Brad struck out across the sands. He was on his way to Wolf's Head Point.

He couldn't help marveling, as he trudged along, how much his visit had already done to build his strength. He'd almost forgotten about the old virus. Aunt Cary's bathroom scales recorded a gain in weight of five pounds, and he felt equal to anything today. Ever since that first night, when he had stood at the water's edge looking across at it, he had wanted to explore Wolf's Head Point. This afternoon seemed the time. So here he was.

At the first pile of rocks, where he and Cricket had eaten their lunch that day, he stopped to rest. No use overdoing things. Besides, he loved to watch the high, green, quivering walls of water fling themselves upon the shore in a never-ending feud with the land. Rested, he began again to climb across the rocks, pausing occasionally to inspect a tide pool.

By thus climbing and walking, interspersed with resting, he came at last to the shores of Wolf's Head Point and entered into its pine forest. A trail under the trees took him across a short arm of land and to a small cove cut into the side of the point. This was Wild Cat Cove, once a famous anchorage for smugglers. Here the pines withdrew from the shore and huge rocks rose up, sheltering the bottom of the cove from view.

Brad left the trail and went to the edge of the cliff to inspect the cove more closely. When he reached the edge and looked down, he gave a surprised start.

The cliff here was a sheer rock wall dropping into a basin of quiet water. All around were rocks, but, on looking across the cove, he could see that the rock wall was broken in such a way as to form a series of giant steps from the water to the top of the cliff. At the foot of this natural staircase, tied securely to a jutting piece of rock, was a boat. It was a fair-sized cabin cruiser with trim lines, paint fresh and clean, and quite the neatest craft Brad had ever seen on TV or off it.

Beyond the cove more rocks loomed and the sea crashed against them, throwing its spray now and then onto the quiet surface of the water inside the cove. Peering sharply, Brad could see an opening between the rocks. It looked just large enough to accommodate the boat below him.

For several minutes he rested on the cliff and let his eyes feast upon the lovely boat rising and falling as the water heaved gently under it. He longed for a closer look.

Getting to his feet, he called down to the boat, "Hello, down there." He waited for someone to appear of whom he could ask leave to go aboard. But only a faint echo from the opposing cliff answered him. He called again, but still without any response from the boat. After a moment's hesitation, he began walking toward the top of the giant stairway.

It was even steeper at close hand than it had looked from the other side. But Brad moved carefully down, watching to see where he placed each foot, and holding to bits of brush and rock along the side. Down, down he went, until at last he was at the water's edge. The boat had moved out about two feet from shore. He stooped to seize the painter and slowly drew the cruiser toward him. It came quite easily for a boat its size. When it was at the shore, he leaped easily into its bow. Grinning with delight, he looked up happily at the granite walls rising all around him. This was something like! Then he turned to inspect the boat.

Whoever owned it was as careful a housekeeper as Aunt Cary, he decided. Every inch of the boat was immaculate. Whatever was metal gleamed, and the paint was without smudge or smear. He went along the deck beside the cabin windows, then jumped down into the waist of the boat and entered the cabin.

Brad's interest in housekeeping was no keener than that of any other boy nearing thirteen. But, looking around this snug little cabin, he thought of how much fun it would be to take care of it. Think of doing your own cooking in this neat little galley! His eyes wandered to the smoothly spread bunks. What fun it would be to be rocked to sleep there!

Suddenly his eye was caught by an object fastened above one of the bunks, and he gave a start of surprise. It was a rifle. Now, as it happened, Brad, while he knew very little about boats, knew a good deal about rifles. He had owned a .22 for two years. He leaned closer to inspect this one and found it to be a powerful gun. His eyes slid to the shelf above the head of the bunk. On it, along with several rounds of ammunition, was a .38 revolver.

Brad didn't like the looks of those guns. Eagerly as he had wanted to come aboard this boat, as eagerly he now wanted to be away from it. Quickly he backed out of the cabin. He reached the deck and started to squeeze his way past the cabin to the bow, when something caused him to lift his eyes to the top of the cliff. What he saw there made his heart jump painfully in his chest.

Two men had been about to start down to the boat at the very moment Brad emerged from the cabin. Now they stood frozen at the top of the cliff and looked fiercely down at the boy who, equally frozen, stared helplessly up at them—helplessly, because there was no room on that stairway for two people to pass, and now the men had started down. One of them looked vaguely familiar, but Brad discounted any possibility that he might know him.

He could do nothing but stand there fearfully and await the arrival of these two strangers, hoping that the expressions on their faces as they came closer didn't mirror their feeling toward him. Why should they resent him so much? All he had done was to come aboard their boat. He hadn't touched a thing; he never would have touched a thing. Perhaps when he had explained this to them they wouldn't look so angry.

"Hi," he called when they were within easy hearing. "This is a real keen boat you've got here."

The first man leaped aboard and grabbed Brad by the front of his windbreaker. "What business you got to be meddlin' around here?"

"You let go of me," cried Brad, hitting at the hand that held him. "I wasn't meddling. I haven't touched a thing and I wasn't ever going to."

The second man stepped into the bow. "You been inside that cabin?" he demanded.

"Suppose I have," said Brad, turning to face him. The first man had released him now and on the tiny deck of the boat the three were almost touching one another. "I didn't mean any harm and I haven't *done* any harm," he said defiantly and met the eyes of the second man. Instantly all terror drained from him. This second man was none other than the driver of the car which had taken him home on that first night when the major had walked him off his feet. It was the man who knew Cricket's grandfather.

Brad heaved a thankful sigh. "Don't you remember me?" he asked.

The man shook his head. "I've never seen you before in my life."

"Yes, you have," insisted Brad, grinning now. "I'm the guy you drove home that night—when I sprained my ankle. You left me off at my aunt's house, Three Corners."

Dawning recognition appeared on the man's face, and he turned to his companion. "The kid's right. I did drive him home. I remember now," To Brad he said, "Get goin', kid, and let this be a lesson to you. Comin' aboard a boat without the owner's permission is the same as goin' into somebody's house without permission. Trespass. Get it?"

Brad nodded, being unequal to anything more. His face was red as a beet and he felt a perfect fool.

"Well," said the man, "don't stand there. Get goin', I said."

Brad went, feeling their angry eyes upon him as he toiled up the giant stairway. By the time he reached the top, he had just breath enough to stagger away from the cliff and beyond the reach of those eyes. Then he fell full length, panting.

In a very few minutes the sound of a motor in the cove below made him sit up. The boat was leaving! He just had to see that boat in motion. It didn't in the least spoil its beauty that two such unfriendly creatures owned it. He refused to worry about the guns he had seen in the cabin. They had looked dangerous and sinister all right, but they might not have been. For all he knew about it, everybody who sailed the sea, even in small boats, carried side arms.

Crawling on all fours, he cautiously approached the edge of the cliff, careful to keep rocks and bushes between him and the water. At last he was close enough to look down into the cove. Yes, the painter had been cast off and the boat was backing into the wider reaches of the cove, her motor whitening the water as she went. Despite the scare she had brought him, Brad watched her with loving eyes, noting with considerable relief that both men were aboard her. The one he had recognized was at the wheel. Slowly the craft turned and headed out to sea, going easily through the channel between the line of rocks.

In a few minutes she was hardly more than a white mark on the blue expanse of ocean. Inside the cove the water, churned by the boat's propellers, was quiet again. Two gulls rode majestically up and down on its gently heaving surface. A third gull stood, a flat-footed sentinel, on one of the rocks forming the channel and looked speculatively out to sea.

It seemed almost ominously quiet after the noise of the boat's departure. Brad drew back from the cliff and looked quickly over his shoulder, but there was nobody behind him. A jay screamed once; then there was silence. During that silence a cone dropped out of a pine close to Brad and hit the ground with a plainly audible thud. The jay screamed again.

Brad got to his feet and looked back along the trail he had come by, trying to decide whether to return home or to do a little exploring first. He was curious as to why those two men had anchored in this cove. The most obvious explanation would be that they lived here. Though there was no house in sight, one could easily be hidden away somewhere among these pines. Brad, who enjoyed a mystery as much as anyone, almost hoped this wouldn't prove true. For it would be only natural that people living on the edge of the sea should have a boat landing, especially when nature had provided such a good one.

But maybe there wasn't a house.

14

THE DESERTED
GRAVEYARD

Brad turned his back on the brightness of the cove and, walking slowly, entered the shade of the pines. His feet were sound-
less on the carpet of needles as he threaded his way among
the trees. He had gone a few hundred yards when the wood
ended and he found himself on the edge of a small meadow.
Across it the pines began again, but less densely. Through
their scraggly growth he could now and then catch the flash
of a passing automobile indicating the presence of a highway.
Beyond that were the hills.

At one side he saw the wood he had left curving to meet
the highway. To his right was a picket fence. So there was a
house after all.

Brad studied the fence before going over to it. It had once
been white, but now most of its paint was gone and many of its
pickets were broken. Weeds were high inside the enclosure,
and it was hard to imagine anyone's living there. From where
he stood Brad couldn't see the house, but of course a house

must be there. A picket fence wouldn't be built around nothing at all!

He started toward the fence, but before he had taken more than a dozen steps he halted and a sheepish smile spread across his face. The picket fence enclosed an old abandoned graveyard.

Well, graveyards were interesting places, especially old ones. Brad reached the fence and leaned against it, staring into the graveyard. It had not been made use of for a very long time. Most of the gravestones were fallen and half buried in sweet alyssum. A few thin slabs of granite still stood upright, but they held no more significance now than visiting cards found in a deserted house. Poppies were everywhere, flashing their bright colors in rather audacious gaiety. Certainly there was nothing spooky about this place, Brad decided, seeking a way through the fence. Two pickets yielded easily to pressure, and he squeezed between them to the other side. As he advanced among the graves, he walked warily, mindful of the bees whose humming rose loud among the scattered clumps of yellow lupine.

It turned out to be a small graveyard. Midway across it he noticed what looked like a little marble house. It was about five feet square with columns marking its door, and Brad recognized it as a tomb. It was the only tomb in the whole graveyard.

"They must have been real important people around here," he said to himself, heading toward it. Of course there would be a name on the tomb, and of course Major Paddleford would know the name and the whole history surrounding it.

He was about twenty feet from the tomb when a sound stopped him and set his heart to racing. The sound was a high falsetto between a whine and a cry of distress. Complete silence followed it, during which Brad didn't move. At last he dared a cautious look around. Everything seemed exactly as it had before. Still he waited, listening. There it came again! This time he was able to catch the direction from which it came. Glancing there, he let out his breath in a long sigh of relief.

Crouched on a fallen gravestone some fifty paces off, his eyes wild and his tail switching, was The Cat.

Brad started toward him, grinning delightedly as one does on discovering an old friend in a strange place.

"How did you get here?" he demanded.

Then his face suddenly lost its look of happy recognition. "What are you *doing?*" he cried, making a dive for The Cat as it reached out and drew an escaping bird to its breast.

"You let that jay alone," cried Brad fiercely as The Cat caught up the bird and started to run with it, his belly hugging the ground.

But Brad was too quick for him. He flung himself at The Cat and managed to grab his tail. The Cat squalled, letting the bird go, and turned to attack Brad. But as soon as he saw the bird flutter free, Brad released The Cat, who instantly diverted his attention from Brad back to the bird fluttering away from both of them.

Carefully Brad stalked it, while The Cat, apparently realizing that it was now lost to him, settled back philosophically and watched the boy's progress.

"You're not a jay after all," said Brad as he drew near to the bird and noted the yellow feathers merging with the blue ones, which weren't really blue at all, but green. In the next

instant he gave a shout as he saw the bird's head clearly for the first time. "You're a *parakeet!*"

At last the parakeet fluttered into a clump of lupine, and there Brad was able to take it into his hands.

"You're hurt," he said, noting the speck of blood on the beautifully penciled breast feathers.

He turned, holding the parakeet, to glare back at The Cat, who still sat calmly on the gravestone, an interested spectator of all that was going on.

"I could kill you," said Brad.

The Cat said nothing, merely continuing to stare at boy and bird, and now and then giving his tail an angry jerk.

Brad cradled the bird against his chest and spoke soothingly to it as his eyes swept the scene around him in a futile search for the home this parakeet must have escaped from. He crossed the meadow to where he could get a view into the trees between him and Crow's Harbor, but there was no sign of a house anywhere.

"The only thing to do is to take you home and put an ad in the paper," Brad informed the bird as he took a close look at it. A bright yellow eye returned his gaze, unblinking. Then the parakeet opened its small curved beak, and Brad could see the thick black tongue inside.

"You want a drink of water, that's what you want," he said and turned decisively toward the pines and the cliff and home. When he came past the graveyard The Cat scrambled up and over the picket fence and galloped after him. Ten paces back of the boy, he slowed his pace to a dignified trot, his tail hanging at about a thirty-degree angle. Thus they journeyed together, the boy and the bird and The Cat, through the pines and over the rocks and across the sands until they reached Three Corners.

Mrs. Cary was sitting in the living room, quietly reading, when Brad rushed into the house, crying, "Look what I found!"

She laid aside her book, took off her glasses, and regarded the excitedly approaching boy with a look of concern. He was holding something in his two hands, and Mrs. Cary didn't altogether trust boys who approached one excitedly with something held in their two hands. It was her belief that boys might be expected to bring home anything from snakes to scorpions. She had no real dread of the latter, never having seen one. But snakes were everywhere, and she was perfectly sure that if Brad should lay a snake in her lap, even one small enough to be coiled in the palm of his hand, she would go right up through the roof and not come down for a dozen light years.

Her relief can then be best imagined when Brad lifted his covering hand to reveal the beautiful parakeet. Boys could be trusted after all.

"Where in the world did you find that?" she demanded.

"At Wolf's Head Point," answered Brad, grinning happily. "Isn't it a beauty?"

"But how did you ever get hold of it? How did it happen to be there?" she asked.

"The Cat had it," explained Brad. "I really took it away from The Cat."

Mrs. Cary gave her head a slight shake as if to clear it. "What would The Cat be doing at Wolf's Head Point and how would he get there?"

"Search me," said Brad cheerfully. "But by golly he was

there and he had this parakeet and I got it away from him just in time."

Suddenly Mrs. Cary snapped her fingers. "He went on the Bookmobile." She looked at Brad eagerly. "Remember we couldn't find him when we got out, and you said he couldn't have been inside because you had looked carefully around before we left?"

Brad nodded.

"Well," went on Mrs. Cary, "he must have been there all the time and when they made a stop somewhere near Wolf's Head Point, he slipped out again."

"I guess so," agreed Brad without much interest. He started toward the kitchen. "This poor bird wants water right away."

Mrs. Cary followed him hastily and unobtrusively substituted one of The Cat's dishes for the Wedgwood saucer which Brad was about to clatter down onto the sink.

At first the parakeet refused to drink, but when Brad picked up the dish and forced the yellow beak into the water, it opened, and the bird drank gratefully.

"What do you plan to do with him?" asked Mrs. Cary.

The question seemed to dampen some of Brad's elation over his find. "Keep him till I find out who owns him, I guess," he said. He spoke dispiritedly and slumped against the sink counter, his eyes hungrily fixed on the gay little body now strutting proudly up and down. Apparently the wound had been a superficial one.

"I sure wish I could keep him for good, though."

"We'll have to put an ad in *The Gull Cry*," said Mrs. Cary firmly. "And in the meantime we will have to protect him from The Cat. And I think that's going to be rather difficult."

"No it won't," said Brad. "We'll just keep him in his cage whenever The Cat's around and remember to close the cat hole when we let him out."

Mrs. Cary looked aghast. "You mean to let him out to fly around the house?"

Brad nodded. "Yeah, sure. These little guys get real tame. They'll ride on your head and even take showers with you if you let 'em."

The parakeet chose this moment to spread its wings and fly straight across the kitchen toward the breakfast table, where it landed on the window sill.

"Something scared him," said Brad.

The Cat spoke from behind them. "You can say that again."

"Oh gosh," wailed Brad. "The kitchen door wasn't shut. But don't worry, I'll catch the parakeet and you get The Cat."

Mrs. Cary looked doubtfully at The Cat, who returned her gaze with a quiet stare, the while he licked his chops.

"I think maybe you'd better take The Cat," she said as the parakeet, seeing Brad's approach, sailed forth again, this time to land atop the stove.

"We've got to get a cage," said Brad, bending to scoop The Cat into his arms. "We've just got to get a cage."

"But where?" demanded Mrs. Cary with some show of irritation. "I don't have a cage and I'm not about to buy one for a parakeet whose owner will claim it in a matter of days."

The Cat turned in Brad's arms to face her. "The attic's full of 'em," he said.

"What?" asked Mrs. Cary, suddenly cupping her face in her hands. Her eyes, round with astonishment, bored into The Cat's.

"You will find bird cages of assorted sizes in the attic," replied The Cat.

"But there *is* no attic," said Mrs. Cary.

Brad chuckled and gave The Cat an affectionate shake. "What are you and Aunt Cary jawing about?" He looked up at his aunt. "What's this about an attic?"

"The Cat says there are some bird cages in the attic, but that's ridiculous because there is no attic."

Brad looked over at the parakeet and back at The Cat. "Most old houses do have attics, don't they?" he said. "Ours does. And it's full of all sorts of junk. If you did have an attic I bet there'd be a bird cage in it, like The Cat said."

"Well, attic or no attic," said Mrs. Cary, "I suppose we must find a cage for that bird, but I'm blessed if I know where."

They all left the kitchen and shut the door on the parakeet.

"I know where," declared Brad, going to the phone. "Major Paddleford can tell us where we can borrow one until we find the owner of the parakeet."

Brad was entirely right. While the major did not himself possess a bird cage, he knew that Mrs. Melton did, or at least had at one time. He knew that Mrs. Crow, who had kept parakeets up to the time of her last illness, had presented Mrs. Melton with one. It had died, and Mrs. Melton had not wished another. But, unless she had sold it, which was unlikely, or given it away, even more unlikely, Mrs. Melton would have the cage and would in all likelihood be willing to lend it to Brad.

"Really," said Mrs. Cary when Brad had hung up and given her the major's report, "really, I am beginning to think that the major is an indispensable member of this community."

Within fifteen minutes after that phone call, Brad had gone across the road and borrowed the cage from Mrs. Melton, who, he said, was very glad to lend it, and the parakeet was installed within it.

There remained now only a trip to the village to buy some bird seed, and Mrs. Melton had told Brad exactly what kind to buy.

15

A CLUE

It was Mrs. Cary who went to the village for bird seed. Brad offered, but halfheartedly; he had had enough walking for one day. Though he would have crawled to the village rather than admit it, the hike across the sands to Wolf's Head Point and back had tired him. Happily for his pride, Mrs. Cary seemed positively eager to perform the errand.

"I've hardly been out of the house all day, and a good brisk walk is just what I need," she assured him, slipping into her jacket and taking her handbag from its hook in the entry closet. "I'll stop in and put the ad in *The Gull Cry*, too. It'll be a few days before the next issue, though."

"That's good," said Brad from the sofa, where he was reclining, the parakeet perched on one of his knees.

"I'm not so sure about that," said Mrs. Cary. "You'll get attached to that bird about the time you'll have to give it up."

"We could get another," suggested Brad.

"We could not," corrected his aunt. "Don't forget his cage

is merely loaned, and parakeets cost more money than either you or I can afford."

"I guess so," agreed Brad, but he spoke without regret, having a strong hunch the ad would never be answered.

As usual Mrs. Cary had a good deal with which to occupy her mind as she walked briskly up the road. Brad had, of course, told her about the boat in the cove, of going aboard it and finding the guns. He had told her, too, about the men and their anger when they discovered him on the boat. She had felt an unpleasant stir of anxiety that one of the men had been the Joe who, with Mo, had come to her house that first night The Cat arrived; the same Joe who, with Mo, had driven Brad home on his first night at Three Corners; the same Joe who, having circled the house several times in his car, had driven her and Cricket to town the day Doc bumped his head. Who was this Joe anyway, and what was he doing at Wolf's Head Point? To the best of her knowledge there were no dwellings there, so he couldn't have been visiting friends.

These thoughts occupied her as far as the Willoughby garden, where they were routed by a hearty "And what takes you to town at this hour of the day?"

"Oh," said Mrs. Cary, yanking herself free of her speculations and pausing to say, "Hello, Major." She was continuing on her way when she remembered that the major had been very helpful a short time ago. "I want to thank you for putting us on to Mrs. Melton. She was very glad to lend Brad the bird cage."

The major, complete with hat and cane, opened the gate and joined Mrs. Cary in the middle of the road. He ran a swift finger across his mustache. "Brad didn't tell me he was expecting to get a parakeet. Did you plan it as a surprise?"

Mrs. Cary shook her head and smiled. "I think my cat planned it. It was The Cat who had it first, you know."

The major's face grew stern and his manner a little withdrawn, as it did whenever Mrs. Cary brought The Cat into their conversations. "I am afraid I don't quite understand," he said stiffly.

"Brad went to Wolf's Head Point this afternoon," Mrs. Cary explained. "There he found an old abandoned graveyard with The Cat inside it holding a parakeet in his claws. Brad made him drop the bird and subsequently caught it. Of course it's somebody's pet. I'm going to town to put an ad in *The Gull Cry* right now."

"You don't say," murmured the major. "How in the world could a parakeet be lost on Wolf's Head Point?"

"I haven't the least idea," said Mrs. Cary, starting to walk on and by no means surprised when the major fell into step beside her. "But there are houses down the highway, and I suppose a bird, even a parakeet, could cover quite a distance if it set its mind to it."

"And what was your cat doing there?" asked the major.

"I really haven't had any opportunity to go into that with him, but I certainly intend to the first chance I get." She spoke quite seriously, and the major gave her a quick sidelong glance. "I can tell you how he got there, though," she went on. "He traveled aboard the Bookmobile. I know he got on it while Brad and I were selecting some books. But I have no notion as to why he should have wanted to go to Wolf's Head Point. It's just beyond me."

The major tried to look amused and gave a tentative chuckle.

"You and that cat," he said. "Forgive me for a personal re-mark, my dear lady, but I am discovering that you have a most original sense of humor."

"I hope you don't mind," said Mrs. Cary quickly.

Lately her feelings toward the major, like her feelings to-ward The Cat, had undergone some change. Though he was certainly a confirmed gossip and a bit of a busybody, she was remembering now as he paced beside her, swinging his cane debonairly, that in all her chatting with him at the mailboxes and on the road to town she had never ever heard the major say an unkind word of anybody. And he had been very kind to Brad, even to locating a bird cage.

Moreover, ever since Brad's return from Wolf's Head Point she had wanted to discuss his adventure there with someone who might be able to throw some light on it. The major might well prove to be that very someone.

"Major Paddleford," she said, breaking the silence that had fallen between them, "can you think of any reason why two men should have a boat at Wolf's Head Point?"

The major's eyes met hers and they shone with interest.

"Just what do you mean, dear lady?"

"Brad found a boat tied up in a cove there and foolishly, I guess, although in fairness let it be said he didn't know any better, he went aboard it. In the cabin, he found two guns, one a rifle and one a pistol. They were in plain sight. This rather frightened him, and he decided to abandon ship. But before he could do so, the owners of the boat appeared and were very angry with him for going aboard. One of the men even grabbed him by his coat, and Brad thought for a moment the man would hit him."

"The scoundrel!" roared the major giving the innocent air a brutal slice. "I'd like to get my hands on him! Why, that boy wouldn't touch a thing that didn't belong to him. I'd bet on that boy to the last ditch. A fine lad! A fine lad! The audacity of that wretch!"

The major's outburst warmed Mrs. Cary, and she let him run on for another minute before reminding him that he had not as yet answered her question.

"Why as to that, my dear lady, I can't truthfully say that I have any idea what they might have been doing there. In the old days rum runners used to go into that cove. It's called Wild Cat Cove, you know."

"No, I didn't know," said Mrs. Cary. "I like the sound of it, though. Wild Cat Cove. Yes, I like it."

"Of course he wouldn't have known who either of the men were," said the major.

"On the contrary. He recognized one of them."

The major's surprise stopped him dead in his tracks. "You *don't* say!"

"It was the man who was driving the car the night you let Brad help you tuck in the neighborhood."

The major stood for a moment, his eyes fiercely blue as they stared into space from under the white ridge of his knotted brows, while his cane beat a tattoo against his leg.

"Well, well, well," he murmured over and over again. "Well, well, well."

Suddenly he began walking, and Mrs. Cary had almost to trot to keep up with him. "That man who was driving the car—" began the major.

"Yes," she said encouragingly.

"I thought I saw him sitting in a car which was stopped in front of your house one evening about a month ago."

Mrs. Cary considered for a moment and then said, "Yes, you did."

"Aha," said the major. "So I was right after all."

"Right?" asked Mrs. Cary.

"Yes, dear lady, right. I never forget a face. This man is the same one who used to call on Mrs. Crow. May I ask what he was doing at *your* house?"

"He wasn't doing anything. The man with him wanted to use my phone after he found out that Mrs. Crow no longer lived at Three Corners."

"Ah, yes," said the major, sounding very mysterious. "Ah, yes."

"What do you mean, 'Ah, yes,' Major?"

"I mean simply that there is something significant in all this. His being with the man who called at your house, then bobbing up again at Wild Cat Cove. I don't like the looks of it somehow."

"Actually, there's nothing mysterious about it at all," she said, trying to sound matter-of-fact. She didn't like the looks of it either, but hesitated to admit as much. To do so might merely confirm the major's suspicions, which actually had little to support them, whatever they might be. "Anyone might call at a house after its owner was dead. And anyone might be at Wild Cat Cove, I suppose."

"With a seagoing craft loaded with guns?" demanded the major. "And why, since this man had been a frequent caller at Mrs. Crow's, why didn't he know she was dead?"

Mrs. Cary, of course, had no answer to these questions and

walked in uneasy silence beside her companion until they came to the village.

"I'm sure if we had the time we could find perfectly plausible answers for all your questions, Major," she said at last, stopping on the corner of the street leading to the pet shop.

"Possibly, dear lady, possibly," returned the major. "Remember, I'll be most interested in any later developments. Most interested." He fixed her with a stern, demanding eye.

"I'll keep you posted," promised Mrs. Cary, at which the major lifted his hat, gave a twirl to his cane, and paced off toward the post office.

She found the pet shop easily enough, being guided to its door by the whimperings of puppies and the whistling of a parrot. The puppies were rolling about on a bed of cut newspaper in the large front window. The parrot sat on a high perch almost in the middle of the store and stopped its whistling to call a cheery, "Hi, there," as Mrs. Cary entered. She turned to reply, saw no one except the parrot, and turned quickly away again, feeling foolish. The counter was at the back of the store, in shadow. Someone was standing facing it, and instantly Mrs. Cary recognized that back and pony-tail. Here at last was Cricket, with Doc at her side.

"Cricket," she called out happily, "how wonderful to find you here. I've called at the motel several times but I haven't been able to reach you. Where have you been?"

"Hi, Mrs. Cary," said Cricket. She glanced up with a fleeting smile of greeting, then dropped her eyes to the counter.

"I've missed you, Cricket. And I have wondered about Doc. How is he?"

Cricket shrugged and threw her another quick smile. "He's okay."

"I'm very glad to hear it," said Mrs. Cary heartily.

Just then a man emerged from the back recesses of the store with a package in his hands. "Here y'are," he said to Cricket. "A dollar ten."

Cricket dug the money out of a coin purse, took the package under her elbow, and, alerting Doc, started away from the counter.

"I wish you'd drop by tomorrow, Cricket," Mrs. Cary called after her. "Brad has a new pet to show you."

Cricket hesitated. "What kind of pet?"

"A parakeet," said Mrs. Cary. "A little beauty, really."

"Well, maybe," said Cricket, adding, "Thanks anyway."

"I'll be looking for you," said Mrs. Cary.

"What can I do for you ma'am?" said the man behind the counter.

There was no chance for further urging of Cricket, and the girl and dog left the store as Mrs. Cary turned to him requesting the brand of bird seed Mrs. Melton had recommended.

"How much?" asked the man.

"One small package," said Mrs. Cary confidently.

"Don't come packaged, just bulk," the man informed her.

Mrs. Cary hesitated, stumped for the moment. At last she said, "Really, I don't know how much I'll need. My nephew found a parakeet this afternoon. It's probably someone's lost pet. I'm going to put an ad for it in *The Gull Cry*, and that won't be out for another week, so I'd want seed for at least that long. How much should I get?"

The man was looking at her with very intent eyes. "Where did he find this here parakeet?" he demanded.

Something in his tone made Mrs. Cary suddenly wary. She returned his gaze with a shrug and a smile. "Really," she lied, "I haven't the least idea. In all the excitement I quite forgot to find out."

The man continued to stand there, looking intently at her, and Mrs. Cary was sure that he hadn't believed a word she said. She never had been able to tell a fib and get away with it. But why had she fibbed in the first place? More than that, why should the man *care* where the parakeet was found?

"What difference does it make, anyway?" she demanded, the color rising in her cheeks. "Did *you* lose a parakeet?"

The man drew up one corner of his mouth with what might have passed for a smile. "No, *I* didn't. But you see, ma'am, we deal in parakeets here, and I know my customers. Might be one of 'em would phone in if they lost their parakeet. If I know about one's been found in their neighborhood, I could tell 'em about you and they could check on the one you found."

Mrs. Cary nodded. It made perfect sense, and she felt a perfect fool.

"Of course," she said, "but the parakeet was found at some distance from the village, near Wolf's Head Point."

"What color is it?" asked the man quietly.

Mrs. Cary looked around helplessly. How did one go about describing that lavishly colored little body? Suddenly, her eyes lit on a cage where sat at least two dozen parakeets colored exactly like the one Brad had found.

"Why, it's like those," she cried. "It's exactly like those."

"And your name, ma'am, just in case somebody should call up?"

"I'm Mrs. Cary. I live at the end of Ocean View Road in a house called Three Corners."

The man wrote it down on a paper bag. "Phone number?" he asked. She gave it. "About that bird seed," he said, going over to some bins along one wall of the shop. "A pound will be plenty. If you run out you can always get more."

Mrs. Cary paid for the seed, picked up the package, and went out of the shop, the parrot whistling at her as she departed.

A car had pulled up beside the curb in front of the shop door, and its driver was getting out. The slam of the car door caught Mrs. Cary's attention, and she looked around in time to see Joe come from around the back of the car and stride into the pet shop.

Mrs. Cary turned away quickly and hurried up the street, her heart suddenly quickening its beat. The sight of Joe coming so soon after Brad's encounter with him frightened her. What business had brought him to the pet shop? Could he have some connection with the lost parakeet? Her steps quickened and she was almost trotting when suddenly she stopped and put her brain to work.

Cricket had been in that shop, buying food for Doc. She herself had been in that shop, buying bird seed. Why shouldn't Joe be going in there for a similar reason? She reached the corner and paused to inspect carefully the assorted articles in The Village Drugstore windows. But though she lingered there for fully ten minutes, Joe never came out of the pet shop. What could be taking him so long? she wondered.

Her next stop was *The Gull Cry* office.

"I want to place an ad for a lost parakeet," she told the old gentleman wearing an eyeshade who left his battered desk to wait upon her.

He slid a pad of paper and a pencil across the counter toward her. "Better write it down," he said and went back to the desk.

Mrs. Cary pondered her message and wrote it down, then crossed it out and wrote it down again. After a few erasures she thought she had it.

"I'm ready with it now," she called over to the old gentleman, who swung around in his squeaky chair and again approached her. After pushing up his eyeshade, he read: "Found.

Wolf's Head Point. Parakeet. Small, blue-green. Call Mayfair 4-2958."

The man looked up from his reading and eyed her sharply. "When did you find the parakeet?"

"Do I have to put that in?" asked Mrs. Cary.

"No," said the man, shaking his head quickly. "Just curious, that's all. There's some parakeet smugglers been operating on this coast off and on for a long time. We ran a piece about it a few weeks back. Wondered if there could be a connection, that's all. Funny coincidence, Wolf's Head Point."

Mrs. Cary leaned against the counter, her legs having suddenly become like well-cooked macaroni. So she *had* read an article about smugglers. And it *had* been in *The Gull Cry*.

"You see, Wolf's Head Point used to be a hideout for rum runners in the old days."

"But why would they want to smuggle parakeets?"

"It's unlawful to bring 'em into this country—parrot disease. Foreign birds are apt to be infected."

"I see," said Mrs. Cary dazedly, drawing slowly away from the counter, and started to leave the shop.

The old gentleman cleared his throat. "That will be a a dollar twenty-five," he said.

She returned hastily, opened her bag, and produced the money.

"Let me know what happens," he said cheerfully as she started again for the door. "You may be in for some fireworks," he added and chuckled merrily at his joke as he settled down again to his worn desk. There was no answering chuckle from Mrs. Cary as the door clicked shut behind her.

All the way home she sifted the conversations she had

had, first with the major, then with the pet-shop man, and finally with *The Gull Cry* owner. She sought to find in them some justification for the fears they had added to the apprehensions already at home in her mind. Long before the cypresses of Three Corners came into view she found herself almost wishing that The Cat had not been frustrated in his attempt to add parakeet to the rest of his diet.

Why *couldn't* The Cat mind his own cat's business? Why did he have to go to Wolf's Head Point in the first place? And just when she was starting to be a little fond of him, too!

16

THE GHOST
WALKS

It wasn't until after dinner that same evening that Mrs. Cary remembered this was the night she had broken her previous rule to permit Brad to watch a night game on TV. But after the events of the day she knew she could never endure an evening alone. Brad was reaching into the entry closet for his windbreaker when she said, "I've changed my mind about your going to the major's. I think you've had enough excitement for one day."

He turned to face her, unbelieving. "Aw, Aunt Cary! What's the idea? I'm okay. Just because I didn't feel like going for the bird seed don't mean I'm sick."

"Doesn't mean," she returned automatically.

"You're right 'doesn't mean,' " said Brad, taking unfair advantage.

"I'm not going to argue with you, Brad."

"But *why?*" he persisted, looking very much like a boy about to bolt in defiance of authority.

"Because I said so, for one thing," she snapped. "For another, I'm not going to let you undo the good your being here has already done you."

"Suppose I decide to go anyway?"

"I shall be bitterly disappointed in you."

There was a note in her voice which Brad had never heard there before.

"I suppose you'd send me back to Kansas," he suggested.

"Would you like that?" she asked quietly.

Suddenly and surprisingly, Brad grinned. "Gosh, Aunt Cary, this is as close to a real fight as we've got."

"And much closer than I enjoy," she replied, her voice a little choked.

Brad took a step toward her. "You aren't going to *cry*, are you, Aunt Cary? Gosh, it's nothing to cry about. Mom and I fight real often, but we don't ever cry about it. It's not that important."

Mrs. Cary turned aside and began to reach blindly in her skirt pocket for the piece of Kleenex that should have been there.

"Aw, Aunt Cary, *honest*," begged Brad, going toward her. Reaching out, he put an arm roughly around her. "I'll stay home. It's okay. Even if it doesn't make any sense, it's still okay."

Still with an arm around her, he walked her back into the living room and sat her down beside him on the sofa. For a moment they contemplated silently the flames moving lazily within the fireplace; then Mrs. Cary spoke.

"Despite what you think, Brad, your staying home this evening does make sense, at least to me. I didn't want to

tell you because I didn't want you to think me a coward."
She looked him full in the face. "You see, I'm afraid to stay
alone tonight."

Brad's eyes looked shocked. "What's scared you?" he demanded.

Choosing her words carefully, and always casting a shadow
of doubt upon any special significance they might have, Mrs.
Cary told him of her talk with the major, of her visit to the
pet shop, and of the conversation with the man at *The Gull
Cry* office.

By the time she had finished, Brad was staring into the
fire with fixed and worried eyes.

"I'm afraid I've frightened you," said his aunt, looking over
at him.

He gave himself a little shake as if trying to throw off
the effect of her recital, then turned a brave but dubious
smile toward her.

"What are you afraid of, Aunt Cary?"

She shook her head and frowned. "I don't really know.
That's what's so frightening, I guess. When you go over it
all carefully, there's no real reason for any concern. You found
a parakeet at Wolf's Head Point. So what?" She thought this
over for a moment then went on, frowning more deeply. "But
you also found a boat with guns on it."

"So what?" demanded Brad. "What's so unusual about
that?"

"Exactly," agreed Mrs. Cary. "How do we know that it's
unusual at all?"

She got up abruptly and began clearing the dinner dishes
from the table, having learned long ago that the comfortable

routines of housework could make almost anything endurable.

"Want me to help?" Brad had squirmed around on the sofa and was now studying her, his chin resting on the sofa back.

She paused on her way to the kitchen and looked sheepishly over at him, "Only for the pleasure of your company," she said.

"Okay." He was off the sofa and over at the table where began such a chiming of silver and crockery as set his aunt to wondering if a whole cove full of smugglers couldn't gain secret entrance to the house under the cover of all that noise and clatter. Just the same, with Brad in the kitchen, the dark beyond its windows would lose its threat—or so she thought. But just as Brad came in, balancing a precarious stack of dishes and silver, Mrs. Cary, who had gone to the sink, let out a shriek. Brad jumped, and the silver cascaded down onto the linoleum. The dishes, though they wobbled dangerously, stayed heaped until he could deposit them on the drainboard, when he saw at once the reason for his aunt's alarm. A face had appeared at the window over the sink. It glowed there against the black velvet backdrop of the night. It was a fairly round face and furry, with two sharp ears pricked attentively above it. As the two startled people watched, the face opened its mouth and both could hear quite distinctly the pitiful cry which came from it.

"Someday I'm going to kill that cat," said Mrs. Cary, furiously turning on the hot-water tap. The steam rose up and wiped out The Cat's visage. But when she turned off the tap, the wailing could still be heard.

Brad was laughing fit to kill. "Honest, Aunt Cary, you sure do have the jumps tonight. You sounded like your throat was being cut." He leaned limply against the drainboard.

"You can pull yourself together and go gather up all that silver you dropped," she returned tartly. "What's the matter with that fool cat, anyway?" she went on. "This is the second time he's perched on a window ledge and startled me out of a year's growth. Why can't he use his cat hole, since he's got one?"

Brad was opening the back door. "I forgot that I fastened the cat hole shut this afternoon when I went over to Mrs. Melton's for the bird cage. I wanted to make sure The Cat didn't get back in while I was gone."

After the conventional amount of coaxing, The Cat permitted himself to enter the kitchen, where he sat down immediately and began going over his coat. Mrs. Cary, shifting pots from the stove to the sink, was forced to walk around him.

"A fine fuss you stirred up today," she said to him on one of her trips.

The Cat left off licking to look up at her. "Things are coming to a head," he announced.

"Just what do you mean by that?" she demanded.

"Not much more than you already know," he told her.

"What made you want to go to Wolf's Head Point?"

"A full belly maketh a happy cat," he murmured, holding up a paw to his mouth. "That's a proverb my father often quoted to us on the rare occasions when he was home."

"I wasn't aware that you felt dissatisfaction with the diet being offered you here."

"Oh, I don't, dear lady. But one likes a snack now and then between meals."

"Wolf's Head Point is rather a long way to go for a mere snack," she said.

"Would you prefer that I hunt closer to home?" He slanted a sly look up at her around his paw.

Mrs. Cary set her mouth firmly and ignored the question.

Brad had been listening with his usual delight at what sounded to him like a one-sided conversation, although his aunt played the game fairly, speaking only after The Cat spoke.

By the time the dishes were done it was nearly nine o'clock, and the fear of smugglers seemed as unreal as the conversation of a cat. With easy good nights they went to their respective beds, The Cat following at Brad's heels.

Several hours later something wakened Mrs. Cary. For a few moments she lay utterly still, hardly breathing. But there wasn't a sound in the house, at least no sound that she could catch above the roar of the incoming tide. Slowly she turned her head upon the pillow to look at the illuminated dial of her bedside clock. The ghostly hands stood at twenty minutes past twelve. It was then she became aware of a peculiar odor. It was rather a pleasant smell and vaguely familiar. But as she lay testing it, her heart began to beat uncomfortably hard and fast. She had never caught this odor before at Three Corners.

She closed her eyes and tried to tell herself that she was imagining it all. It was a bad dream which had wakened her, and this fragrance, for it was a fragrance, was something carried over from the dream. But her heart refused to slow down, and she opened her eyes in time to see a brief flash of light across the high ceiling beams of the living room beyond her bedroom door. For a moment panic seized her and she was sure she would scream. Then reason reasserted itself and she knew that light had come from the last dying flicker of a log settling into the ashes of the fireplace.

She felt the blood slowly returning to her lips, and as warmth again stole through her she realized how great her terror had been. Raising herself cautiously, she reached out and snapped on the bedside light. The room looked reassuringly the same. But the dark beyond the door was like a curtain lowered between her and the unknown, and the strange fragrance persisted, though less strongly now.

She started to swing her feet out of bed. The way to put an end to "the jumps," as Brad had called them, was to reconnoiter and prove to herself that her fears had been groundless. But just as she was about to slip her feet into her slippers a sudden memory hit her with such force that she yanked her feet back into bed and sat huddled with the blankets drawn tight around her. The ghost at Three Corners! Before it walked you smelled sandalwood. Shaking, Mrs. Cary cautiously sniffed the cold bedroom air. To her knowledge she had never smelled sandalwood in her life, and yet this odor had seemed familiar. She was sure now it had been that scent loosed suddenly in the house which had wakened her.

She thought once of calling out to Brad, then put the idea aside as too utterly cowardly. Why scare him half to death in the middle of the night? Summoning all the will power she possessed, she once again lowered her feet out of bed and got them into her slippers. After rising cautiously so as not to let the bed creak, for any sound at all would be upsetting now, she stood up and reached for her robe at the foot of her bed and put it on. She drew its belt around her tightly and slowly went out of the bedroom and leaned for a

minute over the stair railing as she tried to pierce the dark of the room below her. There was no light anywhere. If a falling stick of wood had occasioned that brief flash, it had thoroughly extinguished itself in the ashes, for the hearth was as dark as the rest of the room. She reached behind her for the upstairs light switch and flipped it up. The house sprang into being, and she swept her eyes around quickly, fearfully, but everything looked exactly as it had when she had climbed the stairs to bed over three hours ago. Letting out a deep and thankful breath, Mrs. Cary started slowly down the stairs.

First she put her head into Brad's room. It was too dark for her to see whether or not he was there, so she went in quietly until she stood beside his bed. She put out a hand and felt the reassuring lump of him under the blankets. The

Cat seemed not to be there, and she backed carefully out of the room again.

Next she went into the kitchen, turned on the light, and looked around. It was in its usually spick-and-span condition, smelling faintly of spice, the way a good kitchen should. The electric clock in the stove was growling quietly as was its habit, while the cold-water tap now and then let a long drop splash to the sink. Mrs. Cary, from force of habit, walked over and tightened the tap. It was an old-fashioned tap, and Brad never did take time to shut it off properly. She leaned against the sink while gradually the tension inside her relaxed. Here in this safely utilitarian part of her house, Mrs. Cary had to smile at her previous alarms. Ghosts indeed! That nightmare must have been a dandy!

She straightened up and gave one last satisfied glance around before snapping off the light. It was then her eyes fell upon the one foreign note in her kitchen. On the small table under the window sat Mrs. Melton's bird cage, covered now with part of an old bedsheet. She frowned slightly at this reminder of her most recent apprehensions, then suddenly stiffened. Something was wrong about that bedsheet. She remembered that she and Brad had arranged it very neatly over the cage, making sure that no hint of a draft could reach the parakeet, just as Mrs. Melton had cautioned them to do. But now the cover was slightly awry. Had it slipped during the night? Undoubtedly. Mrs. Cary crossed the room to straighten it. As she took hold of the cloth, she ducked down for a look inside to make sure the bird had come to no harm. She gasped, and the cloth fell from her hand.

The parakeet was gone!

She had had no time to speculate upon this most recent horror when a voice behind her spun her around.

"What's going on?"

There stood Brad, barefooted, in his pajamas, his face stretched in a mighty yawn.

"Oh, *Brad!*" Mrs. Cary sat down limply on a kitchen chair. "You startled me."

"What are you prowling around for?" he demanded.

"Something woke me, and I decided to check. A good thing I did, too. Your parakeet is gone." She was astonished at her ability to keep her voice steady.

"*Gone!*" Brad was thoroughly awake now. In a bound he was over at the cage. "If that cat's got that bird . . ."

"He couldn't have," said Mrs. Cary. "I found the kitchen door closed, just as we left it."

Brad was inspecting the cage, going carefully over every inch of it from top to bottom. Not a wire was sprung.

"Aunt Cary, look!" He was pointing at the door of the cage. "Did you shut the cage door?" he demanded.

Mrs. Cary shook her head. "I haven't touched the cage."

"How could the parakeet get out, then?"

"I don't know." Her voice was hardly above a whisper.

For a moment they stared wordlessly into each other's eyes as the truth dawned upon them. Someone had taken the bird out of the cage and shut the door behind it.

Brad whirled about and started into the living room.

"What are you going to do?" asked Mrs. Cary, following him.

"I'm going to call the police. There are police at Crow's Harbor, aren't there?"

"No, wait, Brad." He was already picking up the phone book. "Wait, Brad. Let's think about this first."

"What's there to think about? The parakeet was in that cage and now it isn't. What's happened?"

"But don't you see, that's just the question? What actually *has* happened? The first thing they'll want to know is how we can be sure that one or the other of us didn't close that cage. You moved it yourself, checking the bars. The door might have swung shut then," she said reasonably.

Brad dropped into a chair and inserted the phone book between his knees as he considered his aunt's words. Suddenly he leaped up, and the phone book slid to the floor.

"Then the parakeet should be in the kitchen," he said, making for that part of the house.

But it wasn't. Together they went over every inch of the room, even poking behind the stove with a yardstick, although it was folly to imagine that such a small space could hold even a small bird. They searched cupboards and looked behind all the canisters. The windows were firmly closed.

"It might have sneaked out when you first opened the door," Brad said, his voice suddenly hopeful.

"Yes," agreed his aunt. "It could have, although I don't think it did."

"Then it might be in the living room," he cried, launching himself upon another hunt.

This time Mrs. Cary refused to cooperate, however. "*If* the parakeet slipped out of the kitchen when I first went in," she said, "it might be anywhere in the house, and I refuse to do any more searching tonight."

A voice spoke from the entry hall. "Very wise, dear lady,"

said The Cat. "And has it occurred to you that it might also have slipped out the cat hole?"

"It wouldn't be likely to push the flap aside, would it?" asked Mrs. Cary.

"No it wouldn't," agreed The Cat evenly. "But it's the unlikely which keeps all our lives from being a dead cinch."

Brad had paused and now stood looking thoughtfully at his aunt. "You know, you're right. That bird could have gone out the cat hole."

"In which case The Cat may have got it," said Mrs. Cary.

Brad looked over at The Cat, who was curling himself up on the sofa, and said, "I don't think so."

"But there goes your case for the police," Mrs. Cary said "Whatever we may think about that bird's disappearance, they are going to want more evidence than we can produce that someone entered this house and took a parakeet. Besides, who on earth would commit burglary in order to get a parakeet, with the pet shops full of them?"

"Yeah," he agreed slowly, but without conviction.

"Let's forget the whole business until morning," suggested Mrs. Cary, starting toward the stairs.

Brad chuckled as he bent to pick up The Cat. "It's already morning." His aunt watched curiously as he stuffed The Cat unceremoniously through the cat hole and fastened the flap down. "If the parakeet is somewhere inside this house, I'm not going to let him make an early breakfast for The Cat."

Mrs. Cary picked up the phone book and put it back where it belonged. Slowly she climbed the stairs. When she reached the top, she stopped and sniffed the air. The faint fragrance still lingered. Then it couldn't have been something she had dreamed. But it couldn't have been a ghost either, she very sensibly told herself.

At that precise moment, Brad's voice came booming up to her from below. "Hey, Aunt Cary. I've just had a great idea."

"Yes?" she called down over the banisters.

"You remember that ghost Cricket was telling you about?"

"Yes"—rather faintly—"I remember."

"Well, I bet it was the ghost that took the parakeet."

She didn't reply at once, and he appeared at the foot of the stairs, grinning broadly up at her. "Well, what do you think?"

"You aren't really serious, are you?"

"Heck, no. Did you think I was?"

"I'm afraid that right now I don't know what to think," she confessed. On an impulse she said, "I wish you'd come up here and see if you can smell anything peculiar."

His grin gone, Brad started up the stairs. "What kind of smell?"

"I'm not sure," said his aunt. "Rather pleasant, though."

Brad had now reached her side and was sniffing in huge intakes, sounding like a dog at a gopher hole.

He shook his head. "Smells okay to me." He looked questioningly toward her. "What's the idea?"

"Don't you remember that Cricket also told me that whenever the ghost walked there was a smell of sandalwood?"

Brad nodded. "She did, all right. I remember now."

"So it couldn't be the ghost," said Mrs. Cary.

"Nope, I guess not." Brad sat himself sideways on the stair rail and began to slide down. "I sure would like to know what happened to that parakeet, though," he called back over his shoulder.

Mrs. Cary turned into her bedroom and began sliding out of her robe. I'm not sure I do want to know, she said to herself. Again she sniffed the air above her bed. Could it be my imagination? she wondered as, shivering slightly, she got into bed and turned out the light.

17

THE SECRET DOOR

Brad spent the next morning searching for the parakeet. He even dismantled the bookshelves he had set up in his bedroom, toppling over the bricks in a crash that brought Mrs. Cary on the run.

"What on earth is going on?" she demanded.

Brad picked himself up from under two four-foot boards and a pile of books.

"Nothing," he mumbled.

She watched for a moment as he dispiritedly replaced the bricks, the boards, and the books, and her eyes were full of sympathy.

"It's too bad about the parakeet, Brad. I'm truly sorry. But I can't help thinking that more is involved here than the mere loss of a stray bird. We're right plunk in the middle of some kind of mystery."

"Maybe," agreed Brad without interest.

"Then let's try to solve it. What do you say?"

He looked quickly around at her. "How?"

She shrugged. "I don't know exactly. But The Cat gave me a clue yesterday—besides bringing home the parakeet, I mean."

Brad got to his feet, the search for the parakeet suddenly forgotten. "What clue?" he asked.

"Remember when we were in the kitchen wondering what to do about a cage?"

Brad nodded.

"And The Cat said there were cages in the attic?" she went on.

Brad frowned and turned away from her to stare out the seaward window. "This isn't any time to kid around, Aunt Cary. You're right, something's going on here. And maybe we could find out what it's all about, so let's not play games."

Mrs. Cary suffered the rebuke in silence and after an awkward moment said, "All right, Brad. But you do remember that we did discuss attics and what one might expect to find in them?"

"Yeah, I remember."

"Well, you know, I think I spoke then more wisely than I knew. There may indeed be an attic in this old house, and I propose that we try to find it."

"How?" asked Brad for the second time.

Mrs. Cary sighed. "The young these days don't seem to have any idea of high adventure. Haven't you ever read about loose bricks in chimneys, of hidden passages and secret doors? Or has all your time been spent on sports and science?"

"Science is high adventure. Darned high," declared Brad stoutly.

Mrs. Cary sighed again. "I suppose. But right now let's think about secret doors and allied topics."

"Okay," agreed Brad. "When do we start? And where?"

"We start immediately, upstairs, of course. Where else would an attic be?"

Together they climbed the stairs. Together they looked long and hard at the walls of the landing outside Mrs. Cary's bedroom. There were two openings in those walls. One led to a closet, the other to the upstairs bathroom.

"The only space big enough to hold a door is right over here," said Brad.

"Very well," said Mrs. Cary. "We'll start searching there."

Carefully she began sliding her hands over the redwood paneling. But Brad reached over her shoulder and knocked against the wood with his knuckles. It gave off a hollow sound.

"There's a door all right," he said. Excitedly he dropped to one knee and began inspecting along the baseboards.

"Look, Aunt Cary. There's a tiny gap along here. This *is* a door, and you enter it by stepping over the baseboard."

He got up and began feeling along the panel joinings.

Mrs. Cary watched him with deep satisfaction. Here was the real Brad restored to her again, eager, interested, a good companion. She was pardonably pleased with herself for having discovered a way of easing the loss of the parakeet. There might or might not be a secret door. In an old house like this one, that hollow sound where Brad had knocked could mean anything, she supposed. But for the moment Brad was happy, and that was what counted most.

"Have you got a flashlight, Aunt Cary?"

"It's in the kitchen table under the window," she said.

Brad slid down the stairs and was back in a jiffy, the flashlight in hand. Carefully he began playing it along one side of the "door."

"Why are you doing that?" asked Mrs. Cary.

"If there *is* a door, then it's been used at some time. Obviously there's no latch visible, but still it's shut. Which means that there's a secret way of opening it. That secret way has got to be at one special spot. So that spot should show more wear than the rest of the door."

"Good reasoning," said Mrs. Cary.

"Scientific," returned Brad.

Suddenly the circular bright light paused and lingered. Then it moved slowly right and left and returned to full stop at the starting point. Brad put two fingers to the spot and pressed. There was a small metallic sound, and a narrow door moved gently back. He looked around at his aunt with a triumphant grin.

"What do you know?" she whispered.

It was a closet all right, but a disappointing one for mystery-solvers. Instead of a walk-in, this closet was scarcely more than a cupboard. It was set above the floor, its own floor level with the top of the baseboards. It was about five feet high and completely lined with smooth wood.

Suddenly Mrs. Cary began to sniff. "Do you smell something?" she asked sharply.

"Yeah," replied Brad slowly. "Now that you mention it, I do."

"It's that closet," she declared. "It's lined with cedar!" Then she gave a little cry. "Why, Brad, that's the odor that woke me up last night. I didn't tell you, but I woke up smelling something. It was a pleasant smell, but I couldn't place it, quite." She laughed softly. "I even wondered if it could be the sandalwood you're supposed to smell before the ghost walks."

Brad grinned. "Is that why you called me upstairs and asked me about it?"

She nodded and smiled back at him. "Silly, wasn't it?"

But Brad had lost his grin and was now soberly looking at the closet. "This could be a clue," he said slowly.

"A clue to what?"

"To the missing parakeet, that's what."

Grim-faced now, he began inspecting the inside of the closet with the flashlight.

"Doesn't it seem sort of funny to you that anyone would have a closet with a secret catch on it?" he asked.

Mrs. Cary thought a moment. "Not necessarily," she said. "Whoever built the house might have traveled a lot and wanted a place to hide valuables and a cedar closet for storing winter things. You must remember that when this old house was built Crow's Harbor didn't have any banks, and hence no safe-deposit boxes."

"I guess so," said Brad from inside the closet. After a series of thumps and knockings, he backed out of it.

"I give up," he said, flinging himself down on the closet floor and leaning back.

The next instant his feet were up in the air and he had disappeared from sight. Mrs. Cary let out a scream and plunged after him. For the next few seconds there was pandemonium as she and Brad tried to extricate themselves from each other and from sticky, tenuous ropes of some eerie substance which

clogged their eyes and mouths and nostrils. At last Brad
gathered his wits enough to snap on the flashlight, revealing
the fact that they had indeed found the attic.

They stood in a small room roughly ten feet square. The
roof slanted low over their heads, and cobwebs hung in loops
and strands and veils all around them.

Off in one corner, neatly stacked one atop another, were a dozen bird cages of assorted sizes.

While Mrs. Cary tried to claw the cobwebs out of her hair and face, Brad swept the flashlight beam up and down and around. But there was no sign of any electric fixture anywhere.

"Let's get out of here," she said, just as the phone began to ring in the entryway downstairs.

Stepping carefully across the secret closet, Mrs. Cary hurried as best she could, while the phone kept right on ringing with maddening persistence. At last she reached it.

"Hello," she said, panting.

"This is Mobray," said a heavy voice at the other end of the line, "Cricket's grandfather. Mind if I come out and talk to you for a few minutes?"

"Oh, Mr. Mobray . . . Wait till I get my breath."

"Take it easy. I'll wait," came the quietly reassuring voice.

Mrs. Cary panted a few more times, took a deep breath, and turned back to the telephone.

"Yes, of course, Mr. Mobray. I wish you would come out. I want to talk to you. And bring Cricket with you, please, and Doc—especially Doc."

There was a chuckle along the wire. "I understand. And I'll bring 'em."

Mrs. Cary hung up and went out to the kitchen to the broom closet. Imagine any room in her house, even the attic, having all those cobwebs in it!

She had tied up her hair and had begun debating with the spiders for the honor of the attic when her callers announced themselves.

"You go let them in, Brad, while I tidy up a bit," she said, and Brad went down to let them in.

By the time Mrs. Cary had washed up and tidied her hair and come downstairs, he had told Mr. Mobray and the silently listening Cricket all about the alarms of the night and the disappearance of the parakeet.

"And now we've found a secret closet and a secret attic— full of cobwebs," said Mrs. Cary as she greeted her guests. "And bird cages," she added.

Mr. Mobray didn't look amused, however. "That's all very interesting, but I don't believe the man who was in your house last night was looking for cages—or parakeets, either."

"The man in my house!" exclaimed Mrs. Cary.

Mr. Mobray nodded. "I'm with the F.B.I., Mrs. Cary. We've been watching a certain man for a long time. That's why I dropped in to use the phone that night; we had seen him entering your garden. Joe saw him leave after I came in. We've known there was a gang somewhere near here, smuggling parakeets. After what happened to Brad at Wolf's Head Point yesterday, we knew we'd have to move fast. We got him as he left your house last night."

"And the parakeet?" asked Brad quickly.

"He had it on him, all right. But we'll have to hold it for evidence."

Mrs. Cary took a deep breath. "Then The Cat was right," she said.

"The Cat?" asked Mr. Mobray.

"He said he never did go much on that Joe."

Mr. Mobray smiled. "He was wrong. Joe is one of our agents. He'd have cracked the case long ago except that Mrs. Crow died. That called for some reorganization by the gang, and we had to let them alone until they were operative again." His smile widened as he looked teasingly across at her. "You may remember I never did go much on cats."

"Yes, I remember," said Mrs. Cary absently. They were all silent for a moment, then she said, "Do you think that man might have known about the secret closet and the attic and that I actually *was* wakened by the scent of cedar last night?"

Mr. Mobray nodded. "Yes, he was looking for something. I suspect that Mrs. Crow had quite a sum of money hidden around here somewhere. She left no heirs and died intestate. She acted as a go-between for the smugglers for a couple of years and must have got a share of their take. But if so, it's never come to light."

Cricket took a quick breath and entered into the conversation. "That explains the ghost," she cried. "That man must have come here when Mrs. Crow was sick, and Mrs. Santee smelled the cedar and thought it was a ghost."

Her grandfather looked over at her. "What's this about a ghost?"

Cricket explained, and he shook his head ruefully, then looked up at Mrs. Cary, his eyes twinkling. "From the lips of babes!" he said. "First I ever knew about the ghost, but it all adds up."

"It was because of the ghost that Cricket and I became acquainted," said Mrs. Cary. "She came here inquiring about it, and I snagged her for Brad."

The two children looked quickly at each other and then away again.

Mr. Mobray spoke. "I was a little concerned when I learned

that Cricket had scraped acquaintance with the mistress of Three Corners. I knew there would have to be some kind of showdown and that it would probably take place here, and I couldn't have her involved. But then I couldn't have prevented her involvement without tipping my hand. It seemed natural enough that she and your nephew should be friends."

"Only we aren't," said Cricket, grinning. "We just naturally hate each other."

"Says who?" demanded Brad with mock belligerence. Then turning to Cricket's grandfather, he asked, "Who was the man you caught?"

"The man who owns the pet shop." Mr. Mobray leaned back in his chair and crossed his knees. "You see, after your aunt went in yesterday with the news that a parakeet had been found at Wolf's Head Point, he had to get busy. The jig was up. They were hiding their parakeets in that old tomb out there. Of course we didn't find any when we went there this morning. He might have entered this house simply in order to steal the parakeet, thinking by that to destroy evidence. But I suspect he was trying to locate Mrs. Crow's money. He knew about the secret door and he knew about the attic. He must have. Mrs. Crow hid parakeets there before they began using the deserted graveyard. He told us that much."

"Then," began Brad, "if The Cat hadn't got aboard the Bookmobile and traveled out to Wolf's Head Point, and if he hadn't somehow got hold of that parakeet, the smugglers might never have been caught."

Mr. Mobray was silent a moment. "That's all highly speculative," he said at last. "We would have caught them eventually. Finding the parakeet did bring matters to a head."

"What about the boat?" asked Brad.

"That's disappeared clean as a whistle," said Mr. Mobray. "But we'll get it, and the man on it. The fellow we've caught will lead us to him before long. They always do."

"Then the Crow's Harbor smuggling case is closed?" asked Mrs. Cary.

Mr. Mobray got to his feet. "Just about."

"But the treasure?" asked Brad. "How about that?"

Mr. Mobray laughed. "We don't know there is a treasure, and anyway the department isn't interested in that. We're only interested in breaking up the ring, and we've just about done that."

"Suppose there were a treasure hidden in this house," said Mrs. Cary, "and suppose I happened to find it. What then?"

Mr. Mobray shrugged as he moved toward the front door. "I'm no lawyer, or at least I haven't been one for a long time now. But I suspect that whatever is on this property belongs to the owner of the property. If you did find a treasure, no one could prove how it came to be here, whether or not it was illegally got, or anything at all about it." He smiled down at her, a teasing look in his eyes. "Happy hunting," he said and opened the door.

Mrs. Cary seemed to be looking inward, for her eyes were fixed unseeingly on the wall before her. It was a moment or two before she roused herself sufficiently to realize that a guest was actually leaving her house.

"Just a moment, please," she said, putting out a hand as if to stop him. "I suppose you'll think I'm very silly, but would you mind if Cricket stayed here with Brad and me tonight? And Doc? Especially Doc. That is, of course, if Cricket would like to."

Mr. Mobray met her question with all seriousness. "That's a good idea," he said. "You'll be safe from prowlers with Doc in the house." Then he smiled. "As for Cricket, I don't think you could get her away from here just now."

Mrs. Cary looked questioning.

"You were too lost in thought a moment ago to notice, but I saw Brad and her climbing the stairs. Unless I miss my guess they're in the attic right this minute, looking for treasure."

"Oh, my goodness!" exclaimed Mrs. Cary. "I haven't even begun to get that place cleaned up. They'll be all over dust and cobwebs."

"And completely happy," said Mr. Mobray as he started down the walk to his waiting car.

But before going to the broom closet, Mrs. Cary took time to make a phone call. She had promised to keep the major informed, and she was a woman of her word.

18

THE TREASURE SEEKERS

The following days were unhappy ones for The Cat. Cricket stayed, and of course Doc stayed with her.

While he knew deep in his cat bones that he no longer had anything to fear from Doc, still the very presence of a dog about the place was unnerving. True, the Doberman spent most of his time in the attic, where his mistress and Brad were going inch by inch over that dusty cubbyhole. But occasionally Doc would get bored with the treasure hunt and come clicking downstairs to stand at the front door and in polite whimpers demand to go out. At these times, The Cat would stiffen where he lay curled on the sofa, ready for an instant take-off if Doc should come into the living room.

During most of the day he stayed safely on the roof of the little front porch. It was from this vantage point that he saw Mrs. Cary on the third morning sally forth, with Doc on his leash pacing amicably at her side. The Cat watched until the pair reached the end of the little walk and turned toward town. Then he rose, stretched, descended from the roof, and disappeared into the house through the cat hole.

For a moment or two he looked carefully around, his tail twitching. Overhead he could hear footsteps and now and then snatches of conversation. Little as he liked the idea of being cornered in the attic when Doc came home, still his curiosity was too great to be denied. Slowly but determinedly he began to climb the stairs. He halted before the secret closet and inspected it thoroughly before placing a paw on its floor. Beyond it he could see a light burning. He stepped cautiously onto the floor of the closet, entered it, and sat down.

In front of him, through the now open back of the closet, he could see Brad and Cricket peering closely at their respective walls. Each was working with a flashlight and a piece of chalk. When they left off to talk to each other, they marked the wall with chalk so as not to miss a single inch.

The Cat watched as Brad made a firm X and turned toward Cricket on the opposite side of the room.

"I'm about ready to give up," he said, sliding down the wall to the floor.

"Well, I'm not," declared Cricket, her fingers pressing carefully, her eyes intent for any telltale crack in the wall she was inspecting.

"We've been over every inch of this hole, wall to wall *and* floor to ceiling. This treasure business is kid stuff. There isn't any treasure."

"Treasure's found every day," said Cricket, "in old stoves, between piles of old newspapers, in books—everywhere."

"Well, it won't be found here," declared Brad.

Cricket made an X and faced him. "And you want to be an astronaut!" she said chidingly.

"What's that got to do with looking for treasure?"

"Everything," said Cricket. "Perseverance, for one thing."

"It's stupid to persevere when you know there's no hope," argued Brad.

"It's also stupid to abandon hope," affirmed Cricket.

"Up to a point, maybe," Brad conceded.

"But how do you know when you've reached the point?"

"You don't," said Brad. "And that's just the point. Anyway, let's quit for a while and go outside."

"Okay," said Cricket.

Unnoticed by either of them, The Cat had entered their shadowy domain and was over in a corner inspecting the stack of bird cages. The children had already inspected carefully the wall behind them and had stacked them up again exactly as they had first found them. Now The Cat was butting his nose along their edges, enjoying the faint smell of parakeet that still clung to them. He never noticed when the boy and girl left the attic, entered the cedar closet, and pressed the spring that swung the back of it tight shut. He was still busy with his inspection, and the fact that he had suddenly been plunged into Stygian darkness affected neither his nerves nor his eyesight.

Left to himself, The Cat continued his inspection. He went carefully all around the walls in search of possible mouse-holes. There were none.

He returned to the stack of bird cages. After some preliminary testing, during which he rose to his full height and placed his paws as far up them as he could, he backed off and leaped up onto them. For a moment he balanced while the stack teetered under him. When he was sure it would fall, he jumped lightly to the floor, and the bird cages crashed down behind him. By that time, however, Brad and Cricket were running wildly up the beach. So the only warning The Cat could have given of his whereabouts was lost upon an empty house.

The hours went by, during which The Cat dozed comfortably. The sun shining down on the shingles of the old roof made the attic warm. The Cat liked the dark and now he knew of a certainty that no dog could find him.

Mrs. Cary and Doc returned from the village. Brad and Cricket came back from the beach, but they didn't return to the attic. Mr. Mobray arrived for dinner, as he had every evening since Cricket's stay at Three Corners. Once Brad asked about The Cat, but no one remembered seeing him.

"I set his dinner out on the back step," Mrs. Cary told him. "He's very much The Cat that walks by himself, but he needn't go to bed hungry."

So the matter rested.

At nine o'clock Mr. Mobray said good night and left. Brad climbed the stairs to bed, for Cricket and Mrs. Cary were occupying the twin beds in his room. Mrs. Cary sat for a while reading beside the hearth, then she put out the lights, covered the fire, and joined Cricket.

Sometime around two o'clock in the morning Brad sat up in bed, his heart racing. He had heard something! Carefully he slid out from under the covers and went to the bedroom door. There he stood listening. Suddenly the sound came again. It was a cat's voice, crying plaintively.

That's funny, thought Brad. If he wants to come in, why doesn't he come through the cat hole?

He went back, got his bathrobe on, and pattered down the stairs. Doc came out of the downstairs bedroom to see what was going on. The clicking of his nails on the bare floor wakened Mrs. Cary.

"What is it, Brad?" she called softly.

"The Cat," said Brad. "He's crying."

"That cat!" grumbled Mrs. Cary, settling back on her pillow. "Now I won't close my eyes again tonight."

Brad opened the front door and peered out. There was no cat in sight. So he went to the back door. No cat there, either. Finally he climbed the stairs again. Now he could hear the sound quite clearly. It *was* The Cat.

All at once he grinned and pressed the secret latch that opened the cedar closet. The sound was plain now. He leaned over and pressed the floor, and the door at the back swung out. There in the light from the landing stood The Cat, his mouth open wide in a loud and pitiful wail.

Brad chuckled and scooped him up as he came through the cedar closet. "So you got yourself shut in, did you? How did you get in there, anyway?"

Mrs. Cary emerged from her bedroom, Cricket coming sleepily behind her. The whole house was awake now.

"What *is* it, Brad?" demanded his aunt.

"The Cat," Brad said, coming down with that animal in his arms. "Somehow he must have slipped into the attic before Cricket and I left there this afternoon, and he got shut in. Poor old guy, I bet he's hungry."

"This house is becoming a perfect chamber of horrors,"

said The Cat. "Vicious dogs, secret passages, rooms you can't get out of. It's enough to make a self-respecting cat look for other quarters."

"Why don't you?" asked Mrs. Cary as Brad reached the bottom step.

He paused. "Why don't you what, Aunt Cary?"

"The Cat was complaining of his present hostelry and hinted that he might find other quarters. I simply asked him why he didn't."

Brad smiled down at The Cat and gave him a little shake. "What do you say to that, old timer?"

"Thanks to my accursed curiosity," replied The Cat, "I think I'll hang around and see what happens next."

"You're not likely to see much excitement from now on," Mrs. Cary told him while Brad and Cricket exchanged delighted grins. "The excitement is all over now."

"You think so!" said The Cat. "I'd advise you to go take a look at that attic."

"But I have taken a look at that attic," said Mrs. Cary. "And Brad and Cricket have been over it inch by inch. There's nothing up there but some old bird cages."

"That's what *you* think," said The Cat and began gently to struggle in Brad's arms. "Will you please tell this kid I want something to eat?"

"He probably wants his dinner, Brad. Suppose you put him out the back door, and then we'll all go up and have a look at the attic."

"At this time of night?" asked Brad over his shoulder.

"Why not?" returned his aunt. "Anyway, after what The Cat said, I couldn't possibly sleep without going up there."

Cricket giggled. "What did The Cat say, Mrs. Cary?"

"Why, you heard him." Then she caught herself and laughed. "I guess after all that's happened I feel a little edgy. Before I return to my bed I want to inspect this house from attic to back steps."

Brad came back from the kitchen.

"Get your flashlights," she said.

They got them; then all three went up the stairs, through the cedar closet, and into the attic. The first things they saw were the bird cages spilled in every direction. The next things they saw were some small flat packages that appeared to be wrapped in white tissue. Brad was on his knees, grabbing for one, his flashlight on the floor at his side. Quickly he unwrapped it.

"Good *gosh!*" he exclaimed, and turned around to his aunt, holding up to view three twenty-dollar gold pieces.

Mrs. Cary was too surprised for speech, but not Cricket. "They must have come out of one of the bird cages, Brad. Let's look."

"I'll hold the flashlights," offered Mrs. Cary, regaining her presence of mind.

In their double beams the two children started toward one of the bird cages.

"Don't touch it," said Brad quickly. "Let's just look at it first, real carefully. Then we'll look at another and another. The gold pieces came out of one of 'em. It may be just a tiny opening, so we'll have to look real sharp. But if we move 'em we might close the opening again."

"What kind of an opening?" asked Cricket.

Brad sat back on his heels and thought a moment. "It would have to be in the floor of the cage." Suddenly he jerked straight.

"That's *it!*" he cried. "I bet they've all got false bottoms. Or anyway some of 'em have."

Very carefully he drew toward him the nearest cage. Slowly, slowly, he pulled out the floor, which in every bird cage is removable in order to be cleaned. All the while Mrs. Cary played the light of the two flashlights full on him. The metal sheet didn't come easily, but Brad worked with great patience to get it loosened. Finally it began to move toward him, and as it came it revealed something beneath. There *was* a false bottom to the cage, and it was filled with United States currency in thin, neat packets!

The treasure had been found.

There was no sleep at Three Corners for the rest of that night. Every one of the bird cages yielded up a sizable sum in either gold coin or currency. By the time all had been inspected and the money gathered up in a paper bag and carried downstairs and counted, it was discovered that something over five thousand dollars had lain concealed in the secret attic.

"The gold coins will have to go to the Treasury Department," said Mrs. Cary when at last their excitement had subsided to the point where they could enjoy a cup or two of hot chocolate. "I don't know much about such things, but I know that no one can keep gold coins."

"Will they give you their value in currency?" asked Brad a little anxiously.

"Oh, yes," said his aunt.

"What are you going to do with the money?" asked Cricket.

Mrs. Cary took a sip of chocolate as she considered the question. Brad had thrown some wood on the hearth, and the three, with Doc, were sitting around the fire, their faces lighted by the blaze.

"I'm not just sure what I'll do with it," said Mrs. Cary. "I already have an idea, but I'd like to think about it a little more." She took another sip. "Usually, when treasure is found, it is used to pay off the mortgage. But that wouldn't be very interesting, would it?" She looked over at the two children.

"No, it wouldn't," said Brad promptly, and Cricket nodded in quick agreement. "Why don't you buy an automobile?"

"Because I have no need for one," she replied. "However, I do think it would be nice to have a small trailer."

"*Trailer?*" he shouted. "What good would a trailer be without an automobile?"

Mrs. Cary's face remained calm as she said, "I've always liked the idea of trailers. Although heaven knows I never want to go trailing in one."

"Then . . . ?" began Cricket, but Mrs. Cary stopped her.

"Let's not talk about it any more tonight." She laughed. "This morning, I should say." She glanced at the clock on the mantel. "Seven o'clock! We've spent nearly five hours finding treasure, counting treasure, discussing treasure. Right now I'm a little tired of treasure. Come on, Cricket, let's start breakfast."

While his womenfolk were busy in the kitchen, Brad again went through the neatly sorted piles of currency and let the gold pieces flow through his fingers. Over five thousand dollars! He had never thought he'd see that much money in his whole life. And yet here it was right on the sofa beside him! What *would* Aunt Cary do with it? *Trailers!* She did have some of the craziest ideas!

19

THE SECOND
LETTER

It was quiet again at Three Corners.

Mr. Mobray had been summoned immediately after break-fast and had taken all responsibility for the details that find-ing treasure on one's property seemed to involve. The treasure itself would be deposited in Mrs. Cary's bank in a special fund awaiting the necessary delays before it could be transferred to her own account. There was no question about her keeping it.

"You deserve a reward anyway for capturing the smugglers," Mr. Mobray assured her.

"But I didn't catch them at all," she protested. "It was The Cat who really led you to them, and you caught the ring-leader yourself."

Mr. Mobray shook his head. "The Cat didn't lead us to anything at all. As I've said, we knew they were using that old tomb to hide the birds in. Joe was there himself and caught Brad coming off the boat."

"That's right, Aunt Cary," said Brad, who was standing

with his aunt on the little front porch, where they were taking leave of Cricket and her grandfather. There was no longer any need for her and Doc to keep guard over Three Corners. With the chief smuggler apprehended and the treasure found, the place could have no further interest for anyone except its owner—or so they thought. Besides, the Mobrays would be leaving soon, now that the case was "broken."

"Just the same," Brad continued, "you've got to admit that it was The Cat who discovered the treasure."

Mr. Mobray laughed. "All right, I'll concede the point, but grudgingly. I still think you and Cricket would have turned it up sooner or later."

They had hardly left when Major Paddleford came pacing down the road. It was almost mail time.

"Can I tell the major about the treasure?" asked Brad.

"I suppose you may," said Mrs. Cary slowly, "but not the exact amount. Just say a few thousand dollars."

"Aw, Aunt Cary," protested Brad, "that wouldn't be polite. Besides, you know what Mr. Mobray said. The newspapers will want full details." His face shone with sudden excitement. "You'll probably be on TV."

"I probably won't!" returned Mrs. Cary firmly. For a moment she watched the major, who was nearly abreast of the garden walk. "Very well, then, tell him something over five thousand. That should satisfy him."

"Hi, Major," called Brad and started down the walk. Then he stopped and turned back to his aunt. "He'll want to know what you're going to do with it," he said softly.

"As to that," said Mrs. Cary, "you may tell him that I intend to buy a trailer with it."

"He'll think you're nuts," declared Brad fiercely.

"It won't be the first time people have thought that of me," replied Mrs. Cary serenely and went back into the house.

Now she was again sitting upstairs at her desk, writing a letter to Amy. Once she stopped her pen's steady progress to go to the window and look down on the group at the row of mailboxes. It was quite clear that Brad had sprung his news story. The major's face was a study in awe, surprise and—she leaned closer to the window—yes, pleasure. You could almost hear his "By jove, dear lady, how marvelous." She went back to her letter.

After a little while The Cat came sauntering in.

"Well, it's nice to have things back to normal again, I must say," he observed before leaping onto the bed.

"But not for long, I'm afraid," said Mrs. Cary, glancing over at him.

The Cat stretched out and, curving a paw in front of his face, he licked it attentively a few times before replying, "You mean the press, I presume. Yes, that will be rather trying for all of us. They'll want pictures, of course. Cat finds treasure. That sort of thing."

"I don't mean that at all."

He stared at her, the paw still curved before his face. "Then what can you mean?"

"Brad's family will be arriving in a matter of days. There will be five of them. That's what I mean."

The Cat sat up quickly. "You're out of your mind."

She smiled over at him. "You know, this all sounds like something that has happened before. I swear those are the very words you used."

"What on earth brings them here?" he demanded.

"The trailer I'm going to buy," she replied smoothly.

"Trailer?"

"Yes, trailer. You know, one of those things you hitch on behind an automobile, that has beds or bunks in it and some kind of cooking arrangement, I presume, and curtains at the windows. Not a big trailer, just one big enough to allow a family of five or six with a little crowding to travel from Kansas to Crow's Harbor without need of hotel accommodations or of restaurants—at least not all the time."

"And what on earth prompted you to want to do a thing like this?" asked The Cat, his eyes wide with horror.

"It suddenly occurred to me that Brad was having a fine time here, and that made me happy. I thought it would make me five times as happy if his whole family were here."

"But how do you know *they*'ll enjoy it?" asked The Cat.

She laughed. "You said that once before too—or I did." Suddenly she grew thoughtful. "Now I remember!" she exclaimed. "It was when I was considering having Brad here and I was thinking out loud and I said, 'How do I know he will be happy here?' and you said, 'You don't,' and it was your saying that which really made my mind up for me."

The Cat glared back at her. "What can I say now to make you change it?"

"Nothing at all," she told him. "My mind is quite made up, and nothing you can ever say again will make any difference."

The Cat jumped down from the bed and stood in the middle of the room, his tail twitching faintly. At last he said, "You have a great deal to thank me for."

The effect of his words could hardly have been predicted, even by The Cat. Mrs. Cary laid down her pen, rose from her chair, approached him resolutely, stooped, and rather awkwardly lifted him into her arms. Then she buried her face in his fur and held it there for several seconds. Why The Cat suffered this strange behavior even he could not have told. Of course his tail slapped against her side, but for a moment he was perfectly still as she held him close.

At last he braced his forepaws against her. Instantly she lowered him to the floor, where he settled his fur before looking up at her. Then he stiffened with astonishment. *Mrs. Cary was weeping.*

"For heaven's sake, what brought that on?" asked The Cat.

She dabbed at her eyes with a piece of Kleenex, blew her nose, and smiled foolishly. "It was what you said," she explained. "I *do* have a great deal to thank you for. You'll never really know how much."

"You mean besides the goldfish?"

"Oh, bother the goldfish! I mean just everything—Brad, Cricket, the smugglers, the treasure, all the *fun.*"

"And the greatest of these is the treasure," observed The Cat cynically.

"That's the very least of it," cried Mrs. Cary. "That's why I'm writing Amy that I want to buy them this trailer. I don't need the treasure; but I do need them. I couldn't bear to let Brad return home if I thought he'd never come back again."

The Cat settled onto his haunches. "I can understand how you feel about that. There never was a nicer kid than Brad." He looked down at his feet for a moment so that his whiskers

204 THE CAT AND MRS. CARY

blended into the fur of his chest. "I don't think I could get along without Brad."

"Then you're willing that I should send Amy a check with this letter and that they should come trailing out here as soon as possible?"

The Cat settled onto his side, laying his head along his foreleg, his whole body suddenly relaxed and sleepy. "Yes, if that's the only means of making sure of Brad, then I give my consent."

Mrs. Cary knelt down and ran a gentle hand along his body. "Let's be friends," she said, smiling tenderly at him.

The Cat made no reply.

Mrs. Cary kept her letter a secret from all except The Cat until she had received Amy's reply. It didn't come as swiftly as that earlier one had, the letter which had been one long hint to have Brad invited to Three Corners. And when at last it did come this second letter voiced so much reluctance and doubt as to the family's wish to accept so handsome a gift that Mrs. Cary put in a phone call to Lawrence, Kansas. This proved to be a wise decision, for even Amy, particularly Amy, could appreciate the extravagance of arguing long distance. In something under seven minutes Brad's mother and father had accepted the trailer and promised to go forth at once and select it. But they couldn't possibly be in Crow's Harbor in under three weeks. Summer session had another week to run, and Mr. Willets was teaching.

During the interval between the letters Three Corners was the scene of continuing activity, but of a different kind. Reporters descended upon the place. Flashlights popped in the attic, and to prevent being photographed herself Mrs. Cary took refuge with Brad and Cricket on the beach, leaving Major Paddleford to act as host at the house. He didn't seem to mind photographers.

The Cat was nowhere around, and the reporters sought him with dogged determination. He had simply vanished when the first stranger came up the walk. The young man from *The Big City Daily* was much put out not to find the cat who found the treasure. But the old gentleman from *The Gull Cry* seemed unruffled at this turn of events, and with reason. Next day, when the excitement had subsided, he came quietly back and snapped The Cat sitting on the end of the walk. The picture appeared on the front page of that week's *Gull Cry*. It was a good picture, for it caught The Cat in a characteristic pose. He was sitting on his haunches, peering around a paw held in front of his nose. It must, of course, have been a trick

of the light, but anyone would have sworn that he was smiling. Mrs. Cary bought several copies.

One afternoon a few days before Cricket and her grandfather were to start driving back to Washington, Mrs. Cary again took the bus to Kingsmount. Beyond telling Brad where she was going, she kept her errand a secret.

She got off the bus at one of the busiest corners on the main street of the small city and went immediately to the nearest jewelry store. There she declared her wish to buy a gold charm bracelet. It was to have a cat, a goldfish, a Doberman, a house, a cage with a bird in it, a smuggler, something indicating treasure, a policeman (that being as close as she thought she could come to an F.B.I. man), and two hearts. One heart was to be engraved with the words "Mrs. Cary." The other was to bear the single word "Brad."

With the help of the clerk, Mrs. Cary found everything she had asked for except the smuggler and the Doberman. However, she decided that a pirate with a wooden leg and a cutlass would do very well in lieu of a smuggler. Hadn't she thought on that night The Cat moved in that Mr. Mobray himself might be a pirate? She smiled as she leaned above the tray of charms. The Doberman seemed a real problem. There were poodles and Dachshunds galore, but nothing resembling a Doberman. Then the clerk produced a catalogue and there, sure enough, was a charm in the shape of Doc. So Mrs. Cary ordered it and went home with the bracelet with all the other charms attached.

On the night before the Mobrays' departure she invited them to dinner along with Major Paddleford. It was a happy affair, and Cricket's surprise and delight when she opened the box at her place and found the bracelet were as real as they were hearty. She squeezed Mrs. Cary until that good woman could hardly draw breath and it was only with the greatest difficulty that she managed at last to quiet Cricket's excitement and explain about the "Doc" charm.

When the time came for good-bys Mrs. Cary found it hard to take leave of Cricket. "You must try to come back next summer when Brad is here," she said, and added, sharing her smile with the two of them, "especially now that you no longer hate each other."

"What do you mean when I'm here?" demanded Brad, his face suddenly hopeful.

"We'll talk about that later," returned Mrs. Cary with just a hint of mystery.

"I'll come back if I can bring Doc," said Cricket with doubtful grace but downright forthrightness.

Mrs. Cary laughed as she leaned to bestow a kiss on Cricket's cheek. "Bring him by all means," she said. "Only please come back again."

She and Brad lingered on the porch until their guests had all got into the Mobray car and had driven off. Then they went back into the house, each a little sad. They would each miss Cricket, and Doc.

20

THE CAT
CHOOSES

It was the day following that farewell dinner that Amy's letter, already referred to, finally arrived and Mrs. Cary placed the call to Kansas. She could hardly wait for Brad to return from watching TV with the major.

When at last he appeared, she delayed lunch to tell him about the trailer.

"It isn't a very personal memento, I'm afraid," she ended, "not at all like Cricket's bracelet. But I thought it might please you more than anything else I could think of. And I know it's what I wish more than anything."

Brad didn't reply at once, and she thought he might be disappointed in her announcement. Could it be possible that he didn't want ever to come back again?

"You see, it's the only way I can be sure of having you here every summer," she went on. "You wouldn't want to spend every vacation away from your family, nor would they want you to." She waited, but when Brad continued silent, she started to speak again. "I thought of keeping the money in a travel fund. But plane tickets for six people would come to an awful lot. A trailer seems the best solution."

At last Brad spoke. "You wouldn't have to spend all the money on a trailer."

"No," she said. "Your parents and I have already gone into that. There'll be about three thousand dollars left over."

"Then you can have your own travel fund," he suggested.

"I don't think I want to travel," returned Mrs. Cary.

"To Kansas, I mean. For Christmas."

"Oh," she said. "Well, perhaps."

He cleared his throat. "Except for The Cat, you're awfully alone in the world, Aunt Cary."

"I suppose I am," she said with a hint of surprise.

"Well, what I want to say is that you're not really alone any more."

She looked questioningly at him.

"What I mean is, you've got me."

Mrs. Cary turned quickly away. "Thank you, Brad. I'll remember that. I'll remember it always."

There was no possibility that anyone unfamiliar with Crow's Harbor could, unaided, find any house in the village. So it had been arranged that as soon as ever the Willets family drove into town they should phone Mrs. Cary. It was on a Tuesday, a half hour before noon, that the call came. Brad's family was down at the service station and would remain there until he caught up with them.

Mrs. Cary had, therefore, about thirty minutes to prepare lunch for seven people. She was in the kitchen, making progress, when Brad's hail, "They're here, Aunt Cary," brought her running to meet them in her kitchen apron. By the time she had gained the front porch, Amy was out of the car and had started up the little walk. She was looking smilingly around her, up at the trees, down at the marguerites, then at last ahead to the house. She saw Mrs. Cary. She stopped and flung her arms wide. And Mrs. Cary, without a word, ran straight into them.

In the next moment Brad's father had swept her into a bear hug, exclaiming as he did so, "What have you done to Brad? Never saw such a change in a youngster in all my life."

Mrs. Cary felt a pull on her hand. "Come and see the trailer," begged Brad. "Please, Aunt Cary, come and see the trailer."

So she went and saw. It was a snug vehicle, almost a house on wheels. But its shiny exterior made the Willets car by contrast seem rather old and shabby.

"Dick and I are going to sleep here," Brad announced. "You and Margaret can have my room, and Dad and Mom can go upstairs."

This was exactly the arrangement Mrs. Cary had already planned on, so there was nothing further to discuss—except, of course, that they would have to get the trailer into the garden somehow. Amy didn't think she wanted her sons sleeping in a trailer parked alongside the road, and Mrs. Cary agreed with her.

Mr. Willets thought an opening could be made in the fence, and Dick and Brad agreed.

"Let's have lunch first," said Mrs. Cary.

So they all trooped into the house—all but Agatha.

"Where am I going to sleep?"

There was extra room in the trailer, but the boys had no intention of having Agatha share their domain.

"There's room for a cot in the downstairs bedroom," said Mrs. Cary.

"Where'll you get one?" asked Brad.

"From Mrs. Melton, naturally," returned his aunt.

And so it was arranged, and Agatha was satisfied.

That was the last meal Mrs. Cary was to prepare during the family's visit.

"I know lots more about cooking for a crowd than you do," said Amy. "Besides, I don't intend to have you waiting on us."

The following days were filled with noise and confusion, with good talk and comradeship. The old house shook to such a banging of doors, such a running up and down stairs, as it had never known before. Fortunately its timbers were well seasoned and its roof conditioned to all the winds that blow, so it took these new buffetings as easily as it had all the rest.

The major was having the time of his life. Each day found him and Mr. Willets setting staunchly forth for some remote destination where cliffs and rocks offered fresh delights to a geologist's heart. Mrs. Cary found wry amusement in these goings-on. She had not suspected that the major's curiosity might reach to ages past.

Then came the day she had been dreading more and more, the day when again the Willets car would be hitched to the new trailer and the return to Kansas begun.

Regardless of his feelings in the matter, she hugged Brad tight and kissed him soundly in front of all his family. And in front of all his family he hastily kissed her back, immediately breaking away to cry, "Where's The Cat? I can't leave without saying good-by to The Cat."

"No, of course not," said Mrs. Cary.

The Cat had adjusted well to the presence of the Willets family at Three Corners. Sometimes he had sought relief on the roof of the front porch from the worst of the bedlam. But on the whole he had borne up bravely, sleeping in the trailer with Brad and dodging safely in and out from among the many feet in the kitchen. Now, however, he was nowhere to be found. He wasn't on the roof; he wasn't in the trailer, where Brad looked for him next; and he wasn't anywhere inside the house, either.

"We can't wait any longer," Mr. Willets at last called out. "You'll just have to drop The Cat a postcard en route."

So, abandoning the hunt for The Cat, they all started to get into the car, all except Brad, who stepped close to Mrs. Cary where she stood at the end of the walk.

"Don't forget you're coming to Kansas for Christmas," he said. Then he scrambled hastily into the car.

Mr. Willets started the motor, and through a chorus of good-bys the car and trailer pulled slowly away. Mrs. Cary watched them almost out of sight, then, turning quickly, she went up the walk and into the house.

The rest of the day dragged miserably, though she managed to keep busy by mopping the kitchen floor, changing the beds, and putting the living room to rights. By the time all was done, the day was pretty well spent and the house was in perfect order once more.

It was while she was getting dinner that she began to feel really lonesome.

At least The Cat will be coming in soon, she said to herself.

But the evening wore on, and The Cat failed to make his appearance. By the time she had finished dinner and washed up the dishes, she was telling herself that he had stayed away like this before. There was nothing to worry about. Only, tonight she wanted him. She was lonely and needed him.

She had settled down by the fire and was trying to lose herself in a book when the phone rang, making her jump. She hastened over to it and lifted the receiver.

"Aunt Cary," came Brad's voice almost before she could say "Hello." "Aunt Cary, something awful has happened!"

"Brad, *what?* What's wrong?" she cried.

"It's The Cat, Aunt Cary. When Mom went into the trailer to fix supper, she found him lying on my bunk. The Cat was in the trailer all the time. He must have hidden himself, because I sure looked hard for him."

"I'm sure you did," said Mrs. Cary, remembering how Brad had checked the Bookmobile.

"Dad says we'll ship him back to you tomorrow."

She was silent for so long that Brad called anxiously, "Did you hear me, Aunt Cary? Are you there?"

"Yes, Brad, I heard you. I think you'd better not ship The Cat back. I think he has made his own choice. In fact he told me once that he didn't think he could get along without you."

Brad's laugh came joyously to her. "You're just as crazy as ever, Aunt Cary. Okay, so I'll keep The Cat. He'll be my memento of the summer." There was a pause. "Aunt Cary."

"Yes, Brad."

"I think you're just super."

Before she could think to reply, the other receiver clicked quietly.

She returned to the fire. So The Cat wasn't coming back, not ever. Suddenly she felt utterly desolate, utterly alone. She couldn't bear it; not this first evening, anyway.

She got up again and approached the telephone table. For a moment she hesitated, then quickly dialed a number. She waited while the phone at the other end rang three times. Finally a hearty "Hello, Paddleford here," smote her ears.

"Major, this is Mrs. Cary. I'm feeling very lonely this evening and I wondered if you wouldn't like to come down for a game of canasta. And I want to talk to you about a kitten."

Had The Cat been lying on the sofa, he would have heard clear across the room the major's joyous "Delighted, dear lady. I'll be right there."

Mrs. Cary hung up and got the card table out of the entry closet.

In no time at all there was a smart rap on the door. She flung it wide, and there stood the major.

"Come in," she cried, and he entered, hat, stick and all. He was puffing a bit, indicating that he had walked briskly, more briskly than usual.

"Now then, what's this talk about a kitten?" he demanded, stalking toward the fire.

"My cat chose to decamp with the Willets family, and I find suddenly that I don't want to live without another. I thought you'd be just the person to know where I can get one."

The major gave his mustache a quick swipe. "As a matter of fact, I do. Mrs. Kane has three she wants to get rid of. But

they're remarkably ugly little things. Of course they're kittens and so they have some appeal and charm. But once they're grown, they won't be any handsomer than that old Tom of yours." He chuckled. "Wouldn't be surprised if he had fathered them."

Mrs. Cary, who had been getting out the cards, whirled on him with delight in her face. "You think so? How perfectly wonderful! I want one of those kittens."

They took their places.

"Can't see why if you're going to keep a cat you don't keep a nice one," said the major, settling onto his chair.

"Cut," said Mrs. Cary.

The major got the deal and began flinging the cards back and forth across the table. Watching idly, suddenly she was seized by an idea, and her face sobered.

"You say Mrs. Kane has three? What will she do with the other two?"

The major shrugged and picked up his cards. "Probably drown 'em. Nobody, except you, of course, dear lady, would want such sorry-looking cats."

She sorted her cards, noting that the major had dealt her three wild cards.

"In that case," she said, "I'll just take all three."

"You're making a mistake," returned the major, but without conviction.

Mrs. Cary smiled. Perhaps, all things considered, it was just as well that The Cat was on his way to Kansas.